How far can you stretch the truth before it snaps?

*What was so terrible about lying? Jessica wondered.
When it didn't hurt anyone and it helped things move
along faster than normal, what was the big deal about
telling a couple of lies? A person couldn't be honest one
hundred percent of the time. If Elizabeth thought she could
be, then she was already telling a lie—to herself. At least
Jessica was truthful about her lying. She didn't pretend
that she was above it.*

*Jessica paused beside her bedroom window and gazed
out at the night sky. Dozens of stars sparkled in the darkness. Jessica searched for a constellation, but she couldn't
find one.*

Elizabeth's words echoed in her head. I don't tell lies.
And I'm never going to. I don't believe in lying. *Did
she have to act so superior about it? Couldn't she see that
once in a while a person* had *to lie? Telling the truth all
the time just didn't work.*

At just that moment a meteor streaked across the sky.
People say that if you wish on a falling star, your
wish will come true, *Jessica remembered.* Well, I wish
Elizabeth would see why you can't tell the truth all
the time. I wish she could see that being a hundred
percent honest isn't all it's cracked up to be!

Visit the Official Sweet Valley Web Site on the Internet at:

http://www.sweetvalley.com

SWEET VALLEY TWINS
◇ SUPER EDITION ◇

Jessica's No Angel

◇

Written by
Jamie Suzanne

Created by
FRANCINE PASCAL

BANTAM BOOKS
NEW YORK·TORONTO·LONDON·SYDNEY·AUCKLAND

RL 4, 008-012

JESSICA'S NO ANGEL

A Bantam Book / April 1998

*Sweet Valley High® and Sweet Valley Twins® are
registered trademarks of Francine Pascal.*

Conceived by Francine Pascal.

*Produced by Daniel Weiss Associates, Inc.
33 West 17th Street
New York, NY 10011.*

Cover art by Bruce Emmett.

ISBN: 0-553-48350-1

Published simultaneously in the United States and Canada

*Bantam Books are published by Bantam Books, a division of Bantam
Doubleday Dell Publishing Group, Inc. Its trademark, consisting of the
words "Bantam Books" and the portrayal of a rooster, is Registered in the
U.S. Patent and Trademark Office and in other countries. Marca
Registrada. Bantam Books, 1540 Broadway, New York, New York 10036.*

PRINTED IN THE UNITED STATES OF AMERICA

OPM   0 9 8 7 6 5 4 3 2 1

To Mia Pascal Johansson

One

◇

"Denny Jacobson is a creep!" Janet Howell announced.

Jessica Wakefield followed Janet's angry stare. Denny was walking across the lawn in front of school, carrying a basketball that he and his friends had been tossing around. Denny had slightly long blond hair, and he was in the eighth grade.

"I wish he'd drop out of school," Janet said, glaring at Denny with each step he took. "I wish I didn't have to look at his face ever again!"

Jessica lifted her eyebrows. For a minute none of the members of the Unicorn Club said a word. She and the rest of the Unicorns were standing in a tight circle on the steps outside school. Janet had called an emergency meeting first thing that morning, before homeroom. Now Janet sounded really upset. As an eighth-grader herself and the president of the Unicorn Club, Janet was always the cool, calm, and collected type. *Besides, weren't she and Denny Jacobson sort of going out until about five minutes ago?*

"I thought you liked Denny," she said to Janet. "Yesterday you said his eyes were as blue as the ocean—"

"His eyes are *hideous*," Janet said, glowering at Denny as he crossed the courtyard in front of Sweet Valley Middle School. "They're not even blue all of the time. Sometimes they're green. They don't make any sense. Just like him!"

"But you said he was the coolest guy in the whole eighth grade," Lila Fowler, Janet's cousin, reminded her. She shifted her red plaid cloth backpack on her shoulder. Lila came from a very wealthy family, and everything she owned had a designer label.

Janet shook her head, and her shoulder-length brown hair swished on her shoulders. "He's a hopeless geek," she said.

"But you said if you could go out with anyone, you wanted it to be Denny," Mandy Miller interjected.

"I'm never going anywhere with him again!" Janet declared. "If he were the only boy in school, I still wouldn't go out with him."

"Wow." Jessica looked wide-eyed at Lila. Lila

was Jessica's best friend, even though they sometimes got into terrible fights. "This sounds serious."

"It is serious. Deadly serious." Janet's blue eyes
narrowed as she drew the group even closer
around her. "He and I were supposed to go to the
Some Crumb Bakery yesterday, after school," she
said in a low voice. "He kept telling me about this
awesome crumb cake they have and how I had to
try it. He said we could hang out there all afternoon. Only he canceled at the last minute, because
he said he had to study for this big science test."
She folded her arms and shook her head. "Yeah,
right. Studying for a science test. As if!"

"What happened? Did he cancel because he was
going out with another girl instead?" Jessica asked.
If so, Jessica would be pretty surprised. Everyone
knew what Janet could be like when she got angry.
Very few sane people would risk her wrath.

"No!" Janet scoffed, acting as if the idea were
completely ridiculous. "Of course he wasn't going
out with someone else. Don't be silly, Jessica."

"Then what are you so mad about?" Mandy
asked, reaching down to tie the laces on her plat-
form oxfords. Mandy was in the sixth grade with
Jessica. She was known for having the most origi-
nal and funky clothes at school. "What *did* Denny
do?"

"One thing's for sure. He didn't go home and
study for a science test, because I saw him playing

basketball with the guys after school instead!" Janet said.

Jessica looked at Lila and made a face. No wonder Janet was so angry. It would have been bad enough to be blown off for another girl, but to be dumped for Bruce Patman, Aaron Dallas, and a basketball hoop? If it had been her, she wouldn't forgive Denny either.

"He's such a liar," Janet continued angrily. "If Denny didn't want to meet me for crumb cake, he should have just *said* so. He didn't have to *act* like a crumb and *lie*."

Jessica doubted that Janet would have been less angry if Denny *had* told her the truth. Janet would have yelled at him for days for breaking their date. Jessica could understand why Denny might have wanted to tell her a little lie. Anybody would have in that situation.

"I am so sick of liars," Janet said.

"Me too," Mandy agreed.

"So am I!" Mary Wallace said. Mary was so friendly and nice, Jessica couldn't imagine her ever lying about anything.

"Oh, yeah. Lying is terrible," Jessica piped up. *Even though sometimes it's the only way*, she said to herself. She thought back to some of the sticky situations she had gotten into in the past and wondered how she ever could have gotten out of them *without* lying.

"And that's why I'm starting this petition against liars." Janet pulled a sheet of paper out of her pink notebook. Then she fished for a pen in her purse.

"P-Petition?" Jessica stammered.

"Yeah. It's an official declaration. It says that anyone who tells a lie can get kicked out of school—not by the principal or the school board or anything, but by general agreement of their classmates." Janet beamed at the group. "Isn't it brilliant?"

"I don't know if Mr. Clark will go for that," Mary said, frowning.

"It's kind of harsh," Mandy agreed. "Not to mention probably against school policy or the law or something."

"OK. How about making the person who lies wear a big, bright T-shirt that says I'm a Liar?" Janet suggested. "And they're not allowed to wear anything else until everyone forgives them."

Mandy smiled. "What color T-shirt are we talking about?"

"The most hideous one we can find," Janet said.

"I like that idea," Mary said, nodding. "But I have a feeling we're going to need about a hundred of those T-shirts."

Ellen Riteman clapped her hand over her mouth. "Oh, my gosh. Can you imagine? Ten people wearing the *same* ugly T-shirt?"

"After a couple of weeks of that, they'll all quit lying," Mary predicted.

"If you really think it's a good idea, then you won't mind being the first to sign." Janet smiled and handed the sheet of paper to Mary. "I bet once everyone sees that the Unicorn Club started the petition, they'll all sign."

"We *are* a major influence," Lila agreed, sweeping her long brown hair over her shoulder. "Give me that pen."

"I hope this makes people think twice before they lie," Mandy said as she signed the petition.

"So do I!" Ellen jotted her name underneath Mandy's.

Janet handed the petition to Jessica. "You're next."

Jessica studied the sheet of paper. She tried to imagine what her life would be like if she could never, ever lie again. What if she got into a tight spot and lying was the only way out? Then what was she supposed to do? Come clean and hope for the best? But that only worked in the movies—and sometimes not even then.

Right off the top of her head, she could think of a dozen times she'd absolutely needed to lie. What about the time she'd told her science teacher that her puppy had eaten her lab report? She didn't *have* a puppy, but Mr. Seigel didn't know that.

And then there was the time she'd told everyone she was going to Paris for spring break. When her parents finally decided she couldn't go, Jessica had lied and said the trip was fantastic—and she'd worn a black beret and brought in a bunch of imported French cheeses to prove she'd gone. She couldn't exist without lies sometimes! Her reputation would self-destruct. And not only that, but if she signed the petition, she might have to wear one of those liar T-shirts. She looked terrible in bright colors. She wouldn't be caught dead in some ugly, cut-rate T-shirt!

"What are you waiting for?" Janet demanded. "You're not actually *deciding* whether or not to sign, are you? Because that would mean you had something to hide, which would mean—"

"Don't be ridiculous. I don't have anything to hide," Jessica said. *At least, not so far today.* "Let's rule out lying for good. Lying is terrible!" She took the pen and scribbled her signature with her right hand—holding her left hand behind her back and crossing her fingers. That way she'd be covered. Technically, she hadn't really given up lying. She was actually telling the truth. And the truth was, she couldn't promise not to lie.

"Then it's settled. Anyone among us who lies . . . well, you're out of the Unicorn Club, for starters," Janet declared. "And after that, it's time for a fashion makeover. You'll be wearing the new school uniform—the liar T-shirt!" She beamed at the group. "If that doesn't make people start telling the truth, nothing will!"

"Good morning." Mr. Davis smiled at the class assembled in homeroom. "How is everyone?"

"Good morning," Elizabeth Wakefield replied cheerfully.

Jessica glanced across the aisle at her identical twin sister, Elizabeth. Sure, she could be in a good mood. She hadn't just had a wake-up call from Sergeant Janet Howell.

Janet was so grumpy, she'd actually demanded that Jessica carry her books to Janet's homeroom, while Lila had to open all the doors for her. Janet was always bossy, though at least she was usually kind of nice about it. But she'd turned into an ogre ever since Denny stood her up. She was worse than the evil stepmother and stepsisters in *Cinderella* combined!

Maybe Elizabeth had the right idea when she decided not to join the Unicorn Club, Jessica thought. At the time, she'd thought her sister was crazy. It just went to show that two people who looked exactly alike—with long blond hair and blue-green eyes— could be completely different. The Unicorns were beautiful and popular. All of Jessica's best friends were in the club. They spent most of their free time doing things Jessica loved, including hanging out, shopping, and talking about boys.

But Jessica and Elizabeth didn't always do everything together anymore. Even though they were identical twins and loved each other more than anything, there were some ways in which they were very different.

For instance, Jessica wore her blond hair down on her shoulders, while Elizabeth tended to put hers into a ponytail or barrettes. Then there was the matter of clothes. Jessica tried to keep up with all of the latest trends, even though it meant spending most of her allowance on fashion. Elizabeth didn't seem to care nearly as much about her looks. She always looked just fine—but she never wore anything anyone would remember the next day, in Jessica's opinion. Jessica was much more interested in making a lasting impression than her twin.

And Elizabeth preferred to spend Saturdays reading or writing rather than hanging out at the mall. She liked parties, but she could live without them. Jessica could understand a lot of things about her twin, but not that! *What's the point of weekends if you don't have eight social events lined up? You might as well be at school,* Jessica thought.

"I have some very exciting news to share with all of you," Mr. Davis said after taking attendance. "Every spring Sweet Valley Middle School hosts a picnic to celebrate the end of the school year."

"Great! Anything's better than math class," Winston Egbert quipped. Winston was always clowning around, making jokes about everything.

"Finally, something worth celebrating!" Mandy added. "No more pencils, no more books—" She glanced at Mr. Davis and flashed her brightest smile. "No more teacher's incredibly handsome looks."

"You are too kind," Mr. Davis said, bowing slightly. "But anyway, this picnic—"

"A picnic?" Lila asked. "Is that all? I thought we'd have a formal party, a graduation, lots of presents—"

"As I was trying to say, it's a gigantic picnic," Mr. Davis explained. "We'll have a large tent, and there will be a delicious buffet with food provided by a catering service—"

"You mean it's not food from the school cafeteria?" Winston interrupted. "Great—we can actually *eat* it!"

Jessica giggled.

Mr. Davis smiled, shaking his head. "That's enough of the wisecracks, Winston. Just think of it as your very own middle-school prom. Without the corsages."

Jessica turned to Elizabeth, her eyes shining with excitement. "A picnic with the whole school? How cool!"

"It sounds great," Elizabeth agreed. "I could use a party right about now."

Jessica grinned at her sister. Maybe she and Elizabeth were more alike than she'd thought!

She closed her eyes for a second, picturing herself in a gorgeous dress. She would be sitting under a tree, picnicking with Aaron Dallas, as all of her friends admired how great she and Aaron looked together. Then the teachers would start handing out awards, and she'd get one for Best Personality, and—

"Jessica? *Are* you here today, or is this just an elaborate illusion?" Mr. Davis was peering at Jessica over the top of his reading glasses.

Jessica felt her face turn red as her homeroom classmates laughed. "I'm here," she said. *In body, maybe. In my mind, I'm already at that picnic!*

Two

◇

"I don't believe it. I can't believe it." Elizabeth shook her head as she stared at the computer screen in front of her. "I just deleted my whole essay!" She was sitting in the computer lab in the school library. Now she'd wasted a whole study hall on nothing!

"We can get it back," Amy Sutton said. She slid into a chair beside Elizabeth and started tapping at the keyboard. "Hmmm. Maybe we can't. What did you save it as?"

"That's just it. I didn't save it." Elizabeth leaned back in her chair and sighed. "Oh, well. It wasn't very good anyway," she told her best friend.

"Yeah, right." Amy rolled her eyes. "You're only the best writer in the sixth grade. Was the essay for

English class? I don't remember Mr. Bowman assigning anything."

"It's for a national essay contest he wants me to enter," Elizabeth said. "I'll just start it again later. Do you want to get some lunch?"

"I thought you'd never ask." Amy picked up her book bag and they started walking out of the library. Todd Wilkins was on his way in.

"Hi, Elizabeth," he said. "Hi, Amy. Where are you headed?"

"Lunch!" Amy said. "And I'm starving."

"Oh. Well, maybe I could go with you guys," Todd said. "I was kind of looking for you anyway." He glanced at Elizabeth. "I wanted to talk to you."

"What about?" Elizabeth asked.

Suddenly Amy started coughing. "You guys go ahead. I need to get a drink of water." She coughed loudly and walked over to the drinking fountain, leaving Elizabeth and Todd alone.

"So what's up?" Elizabeth said, falling into step beside Todd.

"W-Well, I was kind of, uh, wondering, if . . . you know, if y-you want to go to the picnic with me," Todd stammered.

Elizabeth grinned. "That would be great!"

"Really?" Todd asked, sounding relieved.

"Of course," Elizabeth said. She wouldn't tell Todd, but she hadn't planned on going to the picnic with anyone but him. "I'm really looking forward to it."

"Me too." Todd smiled, his face turning slightly red.

Amy jogged up to them, wiping her mouth on the sleeve of her sweatshirt. "Phew. That was some tickle in my throat. I felt like I swallowed a feather!" She cleared her throat loudly.

Elizabeth smiled and shook her head as they all entered the cafeteria. She knew Amy had faked a coughing fit so that she and Todd could be alone. Well, what were best friends for?

"Colin Harmon just asked me to the spring picnic. Isn't that awesome?" Mandy slid her tray onto the table and sat down across from Jessica.

The Unicorn Club ate lunch together at the same table in the cafeteria nearly every day. The spot had been unofficially named the Unicorner.

"That's great," Jessica told her. Mandy was a lot of fun, and she deserved to have a date with someone as cute as Colin.

Of course, he isn't as good-looking as Aaron Dallas, she thought, gazing across the cafeteria as Aaron entered with a group of friends. Aaron was tall, with short brown hair and brown eyes. He was a star player on the school soccer team.

Jessica planned on having Aaron as *her* date. She didn't even want to think about the possibility that he might go to the picnic with anyone else.

"Winston asked me to the picnic during second period!" Grace Oliver said. "Right in the middle of English class."

"How did he do that?" Lila asked.

"Yeah, did he have to raise his hand for permission to ask you?" Mandy asked with a giggle.

"He asked me in writing. He slid me this really cute note," Grace said, smiling. "Actually, he wrote it in the form of a poem. Want to see it?" She showed the piece of notebook paper to the group.

"Knowing him, it's probably a really bad poem," Janet said in a bored voice.

"No, it isn't," Grace said, looking hurt. "He rhymed 'Grace' with 'beautiful face.'"

Janet rolled her eyes. "Not now, OK, Grace? I'm trying to *eat*."

"Well, I was taking a drink from the water fountain and Peter Burns was standing behind me in line," Mary said. "When I stood up, Peter asked if I'd go with him. I was so shocked, I almost choked on the water in my mouth!"

"Peter Burns, suave as always," Janet said dryly.

Jessica frowned at her. Maybe Peter Burns wasn't the coolest guy in school, but if Mary liked him, then Janet shouldn't make fun of him.

"Jim Sturbridge was waiting at my locker after homeroom," Ellen said. "He said he knew about the picnic beforehand, because he'd overheard Mr. Clark talking about it. He said he was planning to ask me ever since yesterday. Can you believe it?" Ellen grinned.

"No," Janet grumbled, "I don't believe it. I'm sure he made that up just to impress you."

"Oh." Ellen's face fell. "Really?"

"Wait a minute," Lila said, looking around the table with a worried expression on her face. "Wait a minute! Does *everyone* have a date to the picnic already? Am I the only one who hasn't been asked yet?"

"No," Jessica mumbled, staring into her juice carton.

"No," Janet muttered.

"Phew," Lila sighed with relief, flipping her long brown hair over her shoulder. "I was starting to worry for a second there."

"So who do you guys want to go with?" Mandy asked. "Wait—don't tell me. Jessica, I'm sure you want to go with Aaron. And Lila, I bet you want to go with . . . Bruce!"

"Exactly," both Lila and Jessica said at once.

"Well, don't sweat it," Mary advised. "I'm sure they'll ask you sometime today. Probably during lunch."

Jessica looked across the cafeteria. Aaron's back was to her as he sat at a table with Bruce Patman and some of the other guys. They were joking around and laughing as they tossed a lime Jell-O cube around. Aaron and Bruce sure didn't seem as if they were busily plotting romantic ways of asking girls out. In fact, she'd have bet it was one of the last things on their minds—if it was on their minds at all.

"So, Janet. Do you want to go to the picnic with Denny?" Ellen asked.

Jessica winced. Why did Ellen have to bring that up? Janet was in a foul enough mood already.

"With Denny?" Janet raised an eyebrow. "Hardly. I wouldn't go anywhere with him even if he apologized nonstop for the next hundred years!" She jammed a straw into a carton of milk so hard that milk splattered across the table.

"Maybe he does want to apologize," Lila suggested, "only he's nervous and—"

Janet snorted. "Then he should get *over* it. And fast. But even if he did apologize, I still wouldn't go to the picnic with him. I detest him!"

Jessica shifted in her seat. She hated when Janet was in a bad mood. She always did something to make sure everyone else's life was as miserable as hers.

"Well, if you don't want to go with Denny, then why don't you ask someone else?" Ellen asked.

"*Who* else?" Janet complained.

"What about Rick Hunter?" Mandy asked. "He's cute."

"All he talks about is tennis," Janet complained. "Anyway, he's not half as cute as Denny."

"OK, then . . . how about Peter Jeffries?" Jessica suggested.

"Come on. You're not serious, are you?" Janet scoffed. "He's only in the seventh grade. And he's, like, two inches shorter than Denny."

Lila slapped her palm against the table. "I know! I bet Jake Hamilton would kill to go to the picnic with you, Janet. You should ask him!"

"Jake? No way." Janet shook her head. "Look, you guys can quit coming up with this lame list of names. Because I wouldn't go with anyone except Denny. I'd just be wasting my time."

"Not even if Johnny Buck asked you?" Mary said. Johnny Buck was the Unicorns' favorite rock singer. Janet went to his concerts whenever he came to town, and she had all of his CDs.

"Even Johnny Buck isn't as cute as Denny," Janet muttered. "Did you hear his last CD? His voice is all scratchy and weird. Not like Denny's."

Jessica and Lila exchanged worried glances. When Janet started trashing Johnny Buck, things could only go from bad to worse.

Mandy cleared her throat. "This might sound crazy, Janet, but hear me out. Maybe Denny didn't mean to lie. Maybe he was telling the truth at the time, but—" She stopped talking as Janet stared angrily at her. "No, probably not. He was lying through his teeth," Mandy finished.

"Exactly," Janet said. "And if I don't have a date

for the picnic, which is highly likely, since I don't know anyone I like enough to go with, then *you* guys have to hang out with me at the picnic," Janet said, fixing her gaze on Jessica and Lila.

"Well, sure, we'll hang out together," Lila said. "I mean, a bunch of us will sit together and—"

"That's not what I meant," Janet interrupted. "Since you guys don't have dates either, then you can keep me company." She looked straight at Jessica and Lila.

Jessica frowned. Just because Aaron hadn't asked her to the picnic yet, that didn't mean she was about to give up on him!

"But I'm going to have a date," she told Janet.

"Oh, really?" Janet glanced over at Aaron's table. "Come on, Jessica. Do you think Aaron's going to ask you to the picnic when he could go with anyone he wants to?"

"Well, *yeah*," Jessica said, glaring at Janet. Really, Janet could be so mean! No wonder Denny hadn't shown up for their date, Jessica thought. Spending time with Janet could be about as much fun as hitting your head against a brick wall.

"And if Bruce asks you, I'll be very surprised," Janet said to Lila. "Even if he does, I wouldn't trust him. He'll probably back out at the last second with some lame story."

"Why would he do that?" Lila asked.

"Because Bruce Patman's a liar, just like Denny

Jacobson," Janet said. "Why else do you think they're friends?"

"Because they like to hang out together?" Ellen suggested.

"No. Trust me. They're both going to be wearing the liar T-shirt soon. In fact, we should probably put in an order for several extra-large shirts," Janet said. She stared across the cafeteria at Denny. "A *rush* order."

"Did you hear her?" Lila paused in the doorway on her way out of the cafeteria after lunch. "She's lost her mind!"

"No way am I going to spend the picnic hanging around Her Royal Grouchiness," Jessica said.

They both watched as Janet walked away down the hall, the rest of the Unicorn Club following her.

"It would be bad enough giving up a date to hang out with Janet on a regular day," Lila said. "But to miss out on our special school picnic—and Bruce? Forget about it."

Jessica sighed. "She'll make our lives miserable if we don't do it."

"And she'll make our lives miserable if we *do*," Lila argued. "On the other hand, my life's already pretty miserable. I mean, the day that Mary Wallace has a date and I don't—well, something is horribly wrong in the universe."

"Janet's acting like she's a terrorist and we're her

hostages. We can't just give in to her stupid de-
mands," Jessica declared, thinking of a movie she'd
seen on television the night before.

"Right!" Lila declared. "Because if we do, then
she'll just keep on treating us like this."

"If she wants to be so mean, fine, but I'm not
going to hang out with her," Jessica said firmly. "At
the picnic or anywhere else!"

"Neither am I!" Lila agreed again. "But, well . . .
what are we going to do? She's expecting us to be there.
If we aren't, then she'll be even more rotten to us."

Jessica hesitated. She knew Lila was right. Janet
never took no for an answer when there was something she wanted. And she wanted someone to
keep her company at the picnic so that she
wouldn't be all alone.

But did that mean it had to be her? And why did
Janet need both her *and* Lila?

Simple, Jessica thought. *She doesn't!*

"I have an idea," she said to Lila. "Janet doesn't
need us both to hang out with her. So—"

"Oh, no. No way!" Lila shook her head. "I'm not
doing it on my own."

Jessica smiled. "Maybe you are, and maybe you
aren't."

"What do you mean?" Lila asked, narrowing her
eyes and giving Jessica a suspicious look.

"Since Janet only needs one of us to keep her
company at the picnic, I have the perfect solution!"

Jessica announced. "Whichever one of us is asked to the picnic *first* gets to have a date. The other one has to baby-sit Janet!"

Lila chewed her bottom lip. "So only one of us misses out on the picnic. Gee, Jessica, that's so generous of you!"

"Of *me*?" Jessica asked.

"Sure," Lila said. "Because I know Bruce is going to ask me this afternoon. And when he does . . . well, you'll be stuck with Janet. Gosh, you're such a good friend to do this for me."

"For you? Please! I'm doing this for me," Jessica said. "As soon as Aaron pops the question in social studies, you'll be carrying Janet's punch at the picnic!"

"Oh, really?" Lila said.

"Really." Jessica folded her arms across her chest.

"Great, then you're on." Lila stuck out her hand and Jessica shook it.

There was no backing out of the bet now. And Jessica was determined to win!

Three

◇

Jessica stared at the telephone on the dining room wall. *Ring!* she commanded it silently, focusing with all of her brainpower. *Ring right now!*

"Jessica, dinner's ready. Everyone's about to sit down. Did you finish setting the table?" her mother asked, tossing a large bowl of green salad with a wooden spoon and fork. Alice Wakefield was tall, with blond hair.

"Yes, I set the table," Jessica said, concentrating on the phone. She grabbed the receiver off the wall and held it to her ear. There was still a dial tone, which meant the phone wasn't broken. So what was wrong with it?

"Then why do you have all those forks and knives in your hand?" her mother asked, walking past Jessica and placing the salad bowl on the table.

"That salad looks great, Mom," Elizabeth said. "Did you put that homemade dressing on—"

"Mom?" Jessica said, interrupting her twin. "Our telephone number hasn't changed, has it? Or did you guys forget to pay the bill last month?"

"Jessica, what is going on with you?" Mrs. Wakefield shook her head, picking up the napkins Jessica had left on top of the buffet. "I've never seen you so distracted before."

"And that's saying a lot," Steven Wakefield added with a laugh as he strode into the dining room. Steven was the twins' fourteen-year-old brother.

Jessica decided to ignore him. That was usually the best approach when it came to Steven. "I'm just waiting for an important phone call, that's all." She shrugged. "No big deal."

Unless you consider the fact that if Aaron doesn't call me tonight, I'll be stuck with Janet from the Mean Planet at the most important social event of the year. That's all.

"Sounds intriguing," Mr. Wakefield said as Jessica finished setting the dining room table. "Who's calling? The lottery? Hollywood?"

"Another girl with a horn?" Steven teased. He made fun of the Unicorn Club whenever he could. "Are you having an emergency meeting to decide whether to wear your purple capes tomorrow?"

Elizabeth giggled.

"No," Jessica said, slamming down the silverware in front of Steven's place. "We don't wear capes. And not that it's any of your business, Steven, but Aaron is going to call me tonight."

"You mean, he's calling to ask you to the spring picnic?" Elizabeth asked.

Jessica nodded. "He was really busy at school today, so he didn't have time."

"Ri-i-ight." Steven nodded. "I'm *sure* that was it."

Jessica hit him lightly on the head with a teaspoon. "It *was*."

"OK, OK!" He laughed. "Quit hitting me! Brother abuse!" he shouted.

"So what's this about a spring picnic?" Mrs. Wakefield asked, sitting down at the end of the table.

"It's our big end-of-the-year party," Elizabeth said. "It's in a couple of weeks. Mr. Davis told us about it today."

"Oh, yeah—I remember that," Steven said. "We had a ton of fun at that thing. The school really goes all out. Great food, games, music. I went with Bridget Barnes. Boy, was she cute. Too bad she moved to New York."

"Wait a second, Steven. You're telling me you actually got a *date* for the spring picnic?" Jessica asked.

"Yes," Steven said, snapping open a cloth napkin. "Of course."

"I want to see pictures. I want proof. I don't believe anyone would go out with you," Jessica said. She thought a moment. "Then again, she did move three thousand miles away afterward."

"Ahem. *I'm* not the one staring at the phone, waiting for it to ring," Steven replied.

"It'll ring," Jessica said, hoping she seemed confident. "It's going to ring. OK?"

"Whatever you say." Steven shrugged.

"Elizabeth, do you have any plans for the picnic yet?" Mrs. Wakefield asked her.

"Todd asked me to go with him. So I said yes," Elizabeth announced. "We'll probably go with Amy and Ken Matthews."

Jessica sat down, unfolding her own napkin. OK, so everyone did have a date before her. Even Elizabeth's best friend, the drab and boring Amy Sutton. But none of that mattered. As long as *Lila* didn't have one yet, she was safe.

Maybe Aaron hadn't asked Jessica yet because he just assumed she would go with him. Or maybe he wanted to ask someone else. But who? And why would he pick anyone else? Janet's spiteful words echoed in her head: *He can go with anyone, so why would he pick you?*

Because I'm one of the prettiest and most popular girls at school, Jessica told herself. *And Aaron and I go to stuff like this together all the time*.

But maybe she wasn't doing enough. Maybe she

needed to put in a little extra effort where Aaron was concerned. Her social life *was* at stake, after all. A plan began to form in her mind.

"So, besides the picnic news, how was school today? How did the math test go?" Mr. Wakefield asked, turning to Jessica as he took a breadstick out of the basket on the table. "You were worried about that last night."

"Oh, it was pretty easy. Didn't you think so, Elizabeth?" Jessica said.

"Not too bad," Elizabeth said. "But the section on metrics was kind of hard."

"Yeah, sort of. But I'm sure we did fine on it." Jessica didn't want to talk about math tests. She had suddenly realized that she had much more important business to take care of during dinner. If Aaron didn't call that night, she would have to make sure that Aaron asked her to the picnic the next day. *A new outfit,* she thought. *That'll get his attention.*

"Listen, Mom and Dad," she began. "This school picnic is a really big deal. I've already gone through my closet. I have absolutely nothing to wear. I know this is a lot to ask, but I was wondering if I could get some extra money for clothes. Please?" Jessica clasped her hands together and looked pleadingly at her parents.

"Wow. What an appeal," Mrs. Wakefield said.

"I don't know why you're surprised. She asks for

new clothes during every meal," Steven commented.

Jessica frowned at him. "I bet you got new clothes when it was your end-of-the-year picnic." *Even though the outfit I want isn't exactly for the picnic,* she thought, *that's a good argument.*

"Actually, you're probably right, Jessica. I bet we did give Steven some extra allowance to buy something to wear. It's a very special occasion," Mr. Wakefield said. "All right. We'll give you some extra money."

"Yes!" Jessica pumped her fist in the air. "Thank you so much, Mom and Dad—"

"But," Mr. Wakefield continued.

Jessica stopped celebrating, her fist poised above her head. "But what?"

"But that's only if you get a B or higher on your math test," Mr. Wakefield said. "So we know you're putting as much effort into studying as you are into looking good."

"Dad," Jessica laughed. "Of course I am!"

"We'll see." He smiled at her. "As long as you're doing well in school, you've earned some new clothes."

"Then Elizabeth must have earned a ten-thousand-dollar shopping spree," Steven joked.

"I get A's too," Jessica told him.

"Sure. And there's water in the desert—once in a while," Steven said with a superior smile.

Jessica felt like leaping across the table and

pinning Steven to the ground. But she took a deep breath and reached for the salad instead. *Who cares about Steven? As long as I aced that math test, nothing else matters!*

Elizabeth handed Jessica a large saucepan to dry. The twins were doing the dishes in the kitchen. Jessica was just about finished when the doorbell rang.

She dropped the saucepan back into the soapy water, let the dishtowel fall to the floor, and raced for the door.

"Hey!" Elizabeth cried. "Now I have to wash that all over again!"

"Sorry—it's Aaron!" Jessica called over her shoulder. Her sister couldn't blame her for ditching dish duty when her date for the picnic was at stake. No one was that heartless.

Aaron didn't call earlier because he was coming over to ask me in person! How romantic!

Jessica paused a moment to smooth down her hair, then pulled open the door. A short person wearing a giant, floppy straw hat was standing on the doorstep.

Jessica's heart sank. She didn't know who this was, but it definitely wasn't Aaron. "May I help you?" she asked.

"Jessica! It's me," a voice whispered. Then the visitor slid back the hat.

Jessica stared. The face was familiar. But the hair . . .

"Can I come in? Quick, before anyone sees me!" the figure said, pushing past Jessica into the living room and closing the door behind her.

"*Lila!*" Jessica gasped. "What happened to *you?*"

Four

"Why don't you want anyone to see you? And why are you wearing that silly hat?" Jessica lifted the hat off Lila's head. She stared at Lila's long brown hair. Instead of being straight, it was now curly . . . actually, *frizzy* was a more accurate description. Jessica had a horrible thought. "Lila, have you been struck by *lightning?*"

"No. I got a *perm*. Let's go to your room," Lila said, grabbing the hat and rushing up the stairs ahead of Jessica. "If Steven sees me, I'll never hear the end of it."

"Good thinking," Jessica agreed. As she followed Lila upstairs she wondered what could have possibly convinced Lila she needed to get a permanent—that night?

Bruce, Jessica thought suddenly. *She's doing this*

to impress Bruce—I can't believe she would pull such a dirty, underhanded trick. . . .

Lila sat at Jessica's desk, hunched over, and put her hands over her hair. "Don't even say anything. It's horrible. The perm came out terrible."

"Well . . ." Jessica didn't know what to say. Lila's hair did look like a bad imitation of a poodle. Or was it a mop?

Jessica felt sorry for her friend—but just for a moment. She reminded herself that Lila had gotten the perm in order to win the bet. But there was no way Jessica was going to let that happen!

"You keep hiding your hair," Jessica said, walking over to Lila. "I can't even see it!"

Lila took her hands off her head and looked up at Jessica. Her eyes were wet with tears. "I wanted to change my look. I didn't want to *ruin* it!" she sniffled.

"It's not ruined," Jessica protested. "It's fantastic! All these curls, and the way the cut frames your face, and—"

"Don't bother trying to make me feel better." Lila wiped her eyes on the sleeve of her sweatshirt. "I'm going back to the salon first thing tomorrow morning to get it straightened."

"Why would you do that?" Jessica struggled not to laugh as she walked around Lila, checking out the nightmare perm. *Lila would probably look better if she shaved her head.*

"Because Bruce will never ask me to the picnic now," Lila said. "You know him! He doesn't go out with girls who have bad hair!"

This hair would have to improve several levels to be considered "bad," Jessica thought. *Right now it's hovering at "painful to look at."*

"Lila, don't be ridiculous. You're overreacting," Jessica told her. "It looks fine! And Bruce might be a tad superficial at times, but he's not going to write you off over a hairstyle. Even if it were bad— which it isn't!"

"I'm getting it fixed tomorrow," Lila grumbled.

"Do what you want," Jessica said, "but I wouldn't if I were you." She tossed a few of Lila's curls. "I'm telling you, this looks great! When Bruce sees you, well, how can he *not* ask you to the picnic? Of course, if you get it fixed, then nobody will notice anything, and it'll be just like another day, and maybe Bruce will ask you, and maybe he won't. . . ."

Lila leaped out of her chair and ran over to the mirror hanging on Jessica's bedroom wall. She fluffed her hair around her shoulders. "Do you really think he'll like it?"

"Definitely," Jessica said, her fingers crossed behind her back. "Don't change a *thing*."

"What happened to *her*? Did she get struck by *lightning*?"

Elizabeth glanced up from her spot sitting on the front steps of school. She noticed a familiar figure shuffling across the lawn, trying not to call attention to herself. It was Lila Fowler—and it was obvious she'd gotten a perm. Elizabeth couldn't say that she exactly liked it. But Lila didn't look *that* bad.

"It's like one of those before-and-after pictures—only now she looks like the before picture!"

Elizabeth glanced over her shoulder at the group of eighth-grade girls talking about Lila.

"Her hair looks like a giant mass of noodles."

"I've got a new name for her: Octopus Head."

The girls started laughing.

Elizabeth shook her head. She hated it when people talked about other people so meanly. She scooted over on the steps so that she was closer to Jessica. "Did you hear those girls?"

Jessica nodded, a vague smile on her face as she gazed across the lawn at Lila.

"Well? Aren't you going to do something?" Elizabeth asked.

"Do something?" Jessica repeated. "Like what?"

Elizabeth thought of what she'd do if those girls were talking about Amy that way. "Tell them to be quiet, or get lost, or—"

"You want me to punch them out or something?" Jessica asked.

"No, of course not. But you're Lila's best friend.

Maybe you should tell her what people are saying," she advised.

"No way!" Jessica said. Elizabeth couldn't read the look on her sister's face. "What I mean is, I might hurt her feelings. I'd hate that."

"Isn't that better than having everyone talking about Lila behind her back?" Elizabeth argued. "You should be honest with her. Let her know people think her perm looks bad."

"If I come right out and say her hair looks awful, Lila will be crushed," Jessica objected. "I'd never tell her that to her face. It would be cruel!"

"Well, what *did* you tell her, then?" Elizabeth asked. "Didn't she come over last night to see you?"

"Sure. And I told her hair looks wonderful," Jessica said with a shrug. "What else?"

"Jessica! That's terrible. You're lying to her," Elizabeth said. "I thought you and the Unicorns signed a pledge never to lie again."

"I'm not lying," Jessica said. "I'm just not telling her the whole truth. That's different."

Elizabeth folded her arms. "I don't see how. Jessica, what's going on?"

Jessica fiddled with her bracelet. "Well, Lila wanted her hair to look nice so that Bruce would ask her out, so she got a perm. But it doesn't look nice. So now Bruce won't ask her out."

"And that makes you *happy?*" Elizabeth's eyes narrowed.

"It does when she and I have a bet riding on who gets asked to the picnic first," Jessica declared.

"What are you talking about?" Elizabeth asked. "What bet?"

"It's a long story. But don't worry, Elizabeth. It's not hurting Lila to have a bad hair day," Jessica said. "It's probably the first one she's ever had. And anyway, maybe the perm will grow out nicely—if it ever unfrizzes." She giggled as the bell rang.

Elizabeth shook her head. "You know what, Jessica? You've got a really weird idea of friendship." *If the Unicorn Club is serious about their petition to stop liars, then Jessica is going to be wearing an ugly, obnoxious T-shirt very soon!*

Mr. Glennon stood over Jessica's desk holding the stack of corrected math tests. Jessica happily tapped her feet against the floor, keeping the beat to a Johnny Buck song in her head. Class was almost over, and she couldn't wait to be out of there!

As soon as Mr. Glennon handed her that B, she was off to the mall. Aaron had said he was going to drop by Casey's that afternoon, and Jessica wanted to make sure he saw her there, looking great in an awesome new outfit.

Mr. Glennon slapped Jessica's test onto her desk, his hand covering the grade. He paused for a moment, and Jessica stared at the white sheet of paper. She scanned it quickly. First there were several red checks, for right answers.

Then she got to the middle section of the test—the part all about the metric system. There was one glaring red X. And another. And another.

Mr. Glennon took his hand off the top of the page and moved on to the next desk.

Jessica stared at the place his hand had been. A giant red C was marked there.

"C?" Jessica cried. "C?"

Five

◇

"Please, Mr. Glennon. Please. You have to change my grade!"

Mr. Glennon raised his eyebrows. "I *have* to?"

"Please! I can't get a C on this test. I just can't!" Jessica begged.

"You just did," Mr. Glennon said.

Jessica frowned at him. Did he have to be so flip about it? Why had Ms. Wyler, her old math teacher, left? Why couldn't she have stayed until Jessica finished sixth grade? This was all *her* fault! Did she really have to stay home with her newborn baby?

Jessica chewed her fingernail. She pictured herself watching Aaron dance with another girl at the picnic while she sat on a blanket wearing a hideous, out-of-date outfit and listened to Janet complain.

"Isn't there something I could do to raise my grade? Could I take the test over? Could I do some extra-credit work?" Jessica begged.

Mr. Glennon held out his hand. "Let me see where you went wrong."

Jessica nervously handed the test to him. "Hmmm," he said as he glanced at her multiple-choice answers, "questions fifteen through twenty-five—those were on the metric system, I believe."

Mr. Glennon looked up at Jessica. "Did you forget to study that part?"

"Of course not! I studied it," Jessica said.

"Apparently not very well." Mr. Glennon raised his eyebrows as he glanced at Jessica's answers again. "You got everything else on the test correct. But this section—it's a disaster. Maybe I could let you do some extra-credit work on the metric system."

"And then you'd change my grade? This afternoon?" Jessica asked, clasping her hands together hopefully.

"This afternoon? Well, that's a bit sudden for me," Mr. Glennon said. "I hadn't really thought of a makeup assignment for you yet."

"But Mr. Glennon, I have to have a B on this test. My parents, they're, well . . . expecting it. I told them I did really well on this test. And I'd hate to disappoint them," Jessica said. *And Aaron.*

"All right. Give me a moment. I usually don't

do this, but for some reason your impassioned plea has affected me." Mr. Glennon leaned back in his chair, tapping his fingers together. "To study the metric system, you ought to do some measuring. You especially need work on your metric distances."

"I could run home after school," Jessica said. "I could run a marathon after school! I'd measure the distance in kilometers!"

"That's a bit far, isn't it?" Mr. Glennon asked.

"Well, anything to get my grade up to a B!" Jessica said brightly.

"Perhaps a walk would be better instead." Mr. Glennon suddenly sat up straight. "I've got it! You could go to my house and take my dog, Sparky, for a walk." Jessica knew that Mr. Glennon lived very close to the Wakefields. "You could measure the distance from my house to the park. Measure it in feet first. Then do the conversion and tell me the distance in meters as well. And once you get to the park, you could do several more measurements."

"Several? How many is several?" Jessica asked. The mall did close at nine o'clock, after all.

"I'll make a list." Mr. Glennon pulled out a sheet of paper and started writing. "Measure the height of the statue . . . the circumference of the lake . . ." He jotted down a list of five more things to measure. "This is just great, Jessica. Besides learning something, you'll be doing me and Sparky a big favor—I can't get away today until six o'clock. He has a lot of energy, and he'll go stir-crazy if he's cooped up too long."

Jessica cleared her throat. Mr. Glennon's list was getting longer and longer. It looked like a lot of work. But if it would get the job done . . .

"Let me get this straight, Mr. Glennon. If I take your dog for a walk, then come back here and tell you how far it was in meters, and measure all that other junk, you'll give me a B on the test?" Jessica asked.

Mr. Glennon nodded. "That is correct."

Jessica held out her hand. "Then give me your key and tell me your address!" She had already casually told Aaron that she'd be at Casey's at around four o'clock. She needed to get started right away!

"Sparky! Where do you think you're going?" Jessica fiddled with the leash in one hand and a small notebook in the other. She was trying keep track of the number of blocks they'd crossed. Since they were all the same length, when she got home with Sparky she could convert feet to meters—and *voilà!* Instant B. Instant new clothes!

Sparky was a Jack Russell terrier—white with brown spots. He had so much energy that Jessica was having a hard time keeping up with him.

As they passed Some Crumb Bakery, the door suddenly opened. Jessica gulped as Denny Jacobson walked out, carrying a miniature round crumb cake in his hand.

Sparky started barking and jumping up and down, pawing at Denny's legs.

"Sorry," Jessica said. "It's not my dog!" She struggled to keep Sparky from leaping right for Denny's crumb cake.

"It's OK. He can have a little piece," Denny said. He broke off a small section of the cake and bent down, holding it out to Sparky.

Sparky devoured it with one bite, his tail wagging furiously. He jumped high in the air, then sat on his back legs with his paws in the air, begging.

"I guess he really likes crumb cake!" Denny said with a laugh, feeding Sparky another small piece. "Almost as much as I do."

"Don't give him too much," Jessica advised. "It's Mr. Glennon's dog, and if he gets sick, my grade's going to go down instead of up." She quickly explained the reason she was walking Sparky.

"Well, I'm headed to the park too," Denny said. "I'll walk with you."

"That would be great!" Jessica said.

"Ah-choo! Ah-choo!" Denny suddenly sneezed twice. "Sorry. I've got allergies. They've been horrible all week." He brushed at his eyes, which were watering.

"Here's a Kleenex," Jessica offered, taking one out of her coat pocket. Then she remembered that she was supposed to hate Denny. After all, he had lied to Janet. Then again, Janet wasn't around. With her luck, though, Janet would drive by, spot them together, and demand that Jessica drop out of the Unicorn Club—if Janet didn't kill her first.

But before she could tell him to get lost, Denny started talking again. They started heading down the street, side by side.

"So, Jessica," Denny said, sounding nervous. "Can I ask you something?"

Uh-oh, Jessica thought. *I hope he's not about to ask me to the picnic! If he does, Janet really will kill me!* "Well, uh, sure, I guess," she said uneasily, staring into her notebook of calculations. *But the answer will have to be no—even if Denny is as cute as Aaron. Maybe even cuter . . .*

"Do you think Janet will ever talk to me again?" Denny said, a worried note in his voice.

Phew. That's a relief. I guess. "Well . . ." Jessica wrinkled her nose. "I'm not sure. She said you lied to her. Do you have an excuse for what happened the other day?"

"It's not just an excuse," Denny said, "it's the truth! I didn't lie to her."

"Then how come you told her you were study- ing and then went to play basketball instead?" Jessica asked.

Denny sighed, sounding frustrated. "I told her I had to study for my science test, and that was true. I was *supposed* to have an extra tutoring ses- sion with Mr. Seigel. But he had to cancel at the last second because of a family emergency. I tried to find Janet to see if she wanted to go to the bak- ery, but I couldn't. So I decided to play basketball with the guys."

"*That's* what happened?" Jessica asked. When you heard the whole thing, it was kind of a boring story. It didn't *sound* like a lie.

Denny nodded. "Janet didn't stick around to hear my explanation. She decided I'm a liar and that's that. But I'm not," he insisted.

"I'm sure if you explained it to her—"

"No. Forget it," Denny said angrily. "I'm telling you, I already tried! I can't believe she's that ready to think I'm a jerk! She should know me well enough by now to know that I'd never do some- thing like that."

"Janet's kind of stubborn," Jessica said. "Once she decides you're wrong about something, it's really hard to convince her you're not. But maybe you should keep trying," she urged. *And that way I won't have to hang out with her at the picnic, be- cause she'll be there with you!* "I bet she's cooled off by now. I'm sure she would hear you out."

"No way." Denny sounded adamant. "As far as I'm concerned, right now *she's* the one who needs to apologize to *me*. See you, Jessica." He walked off toward the basketball court.

Don't hold your breath, Jessica thought. *The last time Janet apologized for anything was never.*

Just when she thought she had a chance to repair Janet's horrible mood, she was back to square one. There had to be a way to get Janet and Denny back together. There just had to!

An hour later Jessica breezed out of Valley Fashions, slinging the bag with her old clothes in it over her shoulder. She caught her reflection in the shop's window and smiled. She looked much better now than she had half an hour before, when she'd run home, showed her mother the B on her math test, and collected the money for her new clothes.

She was wearing a short, cute blue dress with tiny white and purple flowers on it, and a brand-new pair of shoes. When she saw Aaron at Casey's in a few minutes, he'd be instantly reminded of the fact that he still needed to ask her to the picnic. Who wouldn't want to be seen with her? He'd have to be crazy not to ask her on the spot.

She walked down the west wing of the mall, trying to hurry without looking as though she was hurrying. That was when she spotted him. The enemy.

Bruce Patman was walking ahead of her—heading straight for Casey's! Jessica picked up the pace, hustling to catch up to him. She couldn't let him get there first. If he asked Lila before Aaron had a chance to ask Jessica, everything she'd done so far would be wasted!

"Jessica!" Bruce said as she tried to pass him. "Where are you going in such a hurry? Wait up—I need to talk to you."

Jessica paused briefly, turning to him. "What about?"

"That stupid end-of-the-year school picnic," Bruce said. He stopped walking and stared at Jessica for a second. "Hey, you look really nice."

"Thanks," Jessica said. "Well, I should get going—"

"About the picnic," Bruce went on. "I was going to ask Lila. But have you *seen* her today?" He shook his head. "She's like the creature from the perm lagoon."

"Well, it's not the best haircut she's ever gotten," Jessica admitted, although she was annoyed. *Typical Bruce Patman. As much as he likes Lila, he's willing to let her lame hairstyle keep him from asking her out.*

Although, Jessica thought, trying not to smile, *that was sort of my plan!*

"Not the best haircut? Jessica, people are calling her Octopus Head," Bruce said in a serious tone. "There's no way I can ask her to the picnic now. So I was wondering if you'd go with me instead."

No! Jessica thought, staring at him with a panicked expression. *Exactly what I didn't plan!*

She didn't want to go with Bruce. What was worse, she knew he was only asking her because Lila was having a bad hair day. She was trying not to feel insulted, but it was hard.

Then again, maybe this wasn't such a bad thing after all, she thought. Once she accepted a date— any date—she'd be off the hook. She'd wanted it to be Aaron, not Bruce, but those were the breaks. Better Bruce than Janet! At least Jessica could be sure that Bruce hadn't asked Lila yet.

"OK, sure," Jessica said. "I'd love to go to the picnic with you, Bruce."

"Cool." Bruce nodded. "Make sure you wear something really great. Someone might be taking pictures."

Jessica rolled her eyes. *What a jerk.* "Bruce, don't I always look great?" she asked. "Don't worry. *I* won't embarrass you."

"See you later!" Bruce said, heading for the mall exit. "I'll call you!"

"Bye!" Jessica replied. She glanced down the walkway toward Casey's. She didn't know if she should still bother going. But what if Lila was there? She needed to flaunt her good news in person.

She was walking into Casey's when she nearly crashed right into Aaron, who was on his way out.

"Jessica!" he cried, grabbing her arm so she wouldn't fall over. "I was starting to think you weren't coming."

"Well, we didn't make a definite plan," she said.

"I know, but you said you'd be here around four." Suddenly he blushed. "I was just hoping I'd see you here," he said. "That's all."

"Oh." Jessica shrugged. *Well, it's too late now, buddy. You should have asked me to meet you here instead of saying you might show up!*

"I have to take off now, because my parents want me home by five," Aaron said. "But before I go, I need to ask you something."

Uh-oh, Jessica thought.

Aaron shifted from one foot to the other, looking nervous. "Would you be my date for the school picnic?" he finally asked.

Jessica stared into his dark brown eyes. *You already have a date*, she reminded herself. *You'll have to turn him down and go with Bruce.*

But she couldn't say no to Aaron, not when he looked at her like that. On the other hand, she knew it wasn't right to say yes. It wasn't fair—to Bruce or to Aaron—for her to have two dates. Nobody in her right mind would do it. It was wrong! It was impossible! The answer had to be no.

"I'd love to go to the picnic with you, Aaron," Jessica said with a big smile.

"Great!" Aaron smiled back at her, and Jessica knew she had done the right thing. So she'd have to juggle two dates. So what? How hard could it be?

The important thing was that she'd beaten Lila to the punch—twice!

Six

◇

"Jessica, I thought you'd never get here," Janet said when Jessica walked into Casey's. "You said you'd be here at four!"

"Oh. Isn't it four?" Jessica asked.

"More like four-thirty," Janet complained. "I've been waiting for you forever. Where have you *been*? How could you strand me here like this?"

Jessica thought about telling Janet that she hadn't promised to meet her at Casey's, but she knew that wouldn't go over very well in Janet's current mood.

"I'm sorry I'm so late. I've been busy," Jessica said, setting down her shopping bag. "First I had to walk Mr. Glennon's dog—"

Janet cast a questioning look at her. "You had to what?"

"Don't ask," Jessica said with a sheepish smile. "Anyway, then I went shopping, and I guess I lost track of time—sorry."

"Is that a new dress? It's sort of cute," Janet commented. "How come you wore it out of the store? You should have saved it for school tomorrow. Or for the picnic."

"I needed it today," Jessica said. *And it worked.* A little too well, maybe, but she'd take success over failure any day.

"You *needed* it?" Janet asked. "Why?"

"Oh, I mean, I couldn't wait," Jessica said. "I liked it so much that I absolutely *needed* to wear it right away." She smiled at Janet. "So are you here all by yourself?"

Janet gave Jessica a look. "Yes," she said. "Thanks for rubbing it in."

"I didn't mean it that way," Jessica said. "I thought Lila was coming with you."

"She did come. She's right behind me." Janet stepped aside and gestured with her thumb to a booth in the back of the ice cream parlor.

Jessica's jaw dropped as she saw Lila and Mike McCluskey sitting in a booth together.

"Guess what, Jessica? They're going to the school picnic together," Janet said.

"Oh?" Jessica said, her voice cracking. Lila and Mike! But *Jessica* was the one who'd liked Mike— before Lila even knew what his stupid name was.

Then again, I do have two dates already, Jessica reminded herself. *I'm not sure I could handle three.*

Anyway, she'd gotten her two dates before Lila even had one. And that meant Lila had to go to the picnic with Janet—no matter who asked her!

"That's terrific," Jessica told Janet, smiling over Janet's shoulder at Mike. What a nice guy—he didn't care about Lila's bad perm. He was probably a much better date to have than Bruce Patman. Too bad it wouldn't matter!

"Yeah. They look so cute together, don't they?" Janet commented with a wistful sigh. "Nowhere near as cute as Denny and I used to look, but . . ."

Jessica looked away, rolling her eyes. Even when Janet was trying to be nice, she still had to point out how much better she was than everyone else.

"Anyway, enough about that loser," Janet grumbled. "You know what this means. Now that Lila's got a date, you're the only one left. So you can hang out with me at the picnic. There's no way I'm going by myself. I mean, it would be so embarrassing."

"Don't worry. Someone will be there for you," Jessica said, patting her friend's arm.

"Yeah. *You,*" Janet replied.

Jessica just smiled at her. *We'll see,* she thought.

"Well, I have to get going. If I hang out here any longer, that creep Denny might show up. I don't even want to share the same oxygen with him,"

Janet declared. She turned and walked out of Casey's.

Jessica bit her lip, wondering if she should go over and tell Lila the bad news right away or wait until Mike left. She didn't want to make a bad impression on him by seeming competitive.

As she turned to look at their booth, Mike stood up. Perfect timing. Jessica's heart started beating faster. She couldn't wait to tell Lila the bad news!

"I'll talk to you later," Mike was saying as Jessica walked over to the booth. "Oh, hi, Jessica." He laughed. "Bye, Jessica. Bye, Lila."

"Isn't he the best?" Lila said, watching Mike leave. "Did Janet tell you the good news? Well, it's good news for me, bad news for you. Mike and I are going to the picnic together!"

"I'm *so* glad you have a date, Lila." Jessica slid onto the bench seat across from her. "But I should probably let you know that I just got one too, and—"

"Yeah, I saw you talking to Aaron outside, a couple of minutes ago," Lila said.

"I'm really sorry," Jessica said, patting Lila's hand. "But it looks like you and Mike won't be hanging out at the picnic together after all. Well, those are the breaks."

Lila didn't look upset. She was actually smiling. *What's she smiling about?* Jessica wondered.

"I'm glad you're not bitter. I mean, hanging out

with Janet could be sort of fun. You guys are cousins, after all, and you have a lot in common. I bet it'll be a blast," Jessica said.

"You're right. I'm sure we would have had fun—*if* Mike hadn't asked me out right after school. But he did," Lila informed her. "Which means that I win the bet."

"Yeah, right. I don't believe you," Jessica said. "You saw Aaron asking me out, so you hurried to get Mike to ask you out—"

"*I* didn't have to do anything," Lila said. She shook her head and her tight brown curls bounced on her shoulders. "Mike asked me on the way out of school, after my last class."

"Says you," Jessica declared. "Do you actually expect me to take your word for it?"

"Call Mandy and Ellen if you don't believe me. They were there. I've got witnesses, Jessica," Lila said smugly. "And you? You've got a date with Aaron that you're going to have to break—for Janet!" She smiled. "Gee, I hope he's not too upset when you tell him you can't go. And *why*."

Jessica felt her right eyebrow start to twitch. She had two dates lined for up the picnic. How was she supposed to break *both* of them?

Stupid Mike McCluskey. Sure, he was cute. But why didn't he care about bad hair? Did he have to be so nice and forgiving all the time?

But as much as she wanted to hate Lila for getting

a date before she did, and Mike for being so considerate, this was all Janet's fault. The only way to get out of this was to find Janet a date. And not just any date. Jessica had a feeling that Janet wasn't going to be happy until she and Denny patched things up. And if they couldn't patch things up on their own, then Jessica would just have to patch things up for them.

"Well, Lila, I guess I should congratulate you," Jessica said slowly.

"Thank you—"

"But I'm not going to," Jessica cut off Lila's reply. "Not yet."

"Why not?" Lila asked. "You don't think you can break our bet, do you?"

Jessica's eyes lit up as she saw Denny walk into the ice cream parlor. He slid onto a stool at the counter.

"I won't have to," she told Lila, quickly getting to her feet.

"What are you talking about?" Lila asked. "You look possessed, like you're in a trance or something."

"I'm about to make Janet's bad mood disappear forever," Jessica said.

"Oh, you do magic now?" Lila teased.

Jessica ignored her, heading for the counter. She had to talk to Denny—as soon as possible!

*   *   *

"Hi, Jessica. Finished your dog-walking?" Denny dug a spoon into a dish of chocolate chip ice cream. *How can he eat so much?* Jessica wondered. *I guess it's because of all of the basketball he plays.* He looked up at Jessica, his blond hair falling into his blue-green eyes. They were still sort of red, from his allergies. But Jessica could see why Janet liked him so much. His long hair kind of made him look like a rock star.

"Yeah, Sparky's home, safe and sound," Jessica said. She leaned on the counter next to Denny. "I'm glad I ran into you again. Janet was just here." She watched Denny carefully, trying to gauge his reaction.

"Is she gone?" Denny asked, glancing over his shoulder at the crowded restaurant.

Two people would never avoid each other so much if they didn't truly like each other, Jessica reasoned. It was a sure sign Denny and Janet still cared for each other. And if they couldn't realize that on their own, she'd be only too happy to help them.

"No, she left about fifteen minutes ago," Jessica said. "But we had this really incredible talk. I told her that I ran into you while I was walking Sparky. And she said that she was hoping to run into *you*."

Denny looked at Jessica and took another bite of ice cream. He didn't seem thrilled.

Jessica leaned closer and whispered, "She'd probably get really mad if she knew I was talking to you about this. Because deep down, Janet's very shy."

"She is?" Denny asked. *"Ah-choo!"* He grabbed a napkin off the counter and blew his nose.

Jessica nodded. "But since I want you guys to work things out, I thought I should tell you. She's really, really hoping that you'll ask her to the end-of-the-year picnic."

"Hoping? I'd call that *dreaming*," Denny said. "I'm not asking her."

"You're not?" Jessica said, surprised by how angry Denny sounded.

"Nope. Not until she apologizes," Denny said. "She owes me a big apology for thinking I'd lie to her."

"Maybe she wants to apologize but doesn't know how," Jessica said. *And that's the truth. I've never heard Janet apologize for anything in her life!* "She might not know what to say to you."

"It doesn't have to be perfect or anything." Denny stirred his melting ice cream with the spoon. "But she has to say something. I don't even want to talk to her until she realizes how off base she was." He picked up another napkin and wiped his eyes, which were watering. "I might not do everything right all the time. But I'm no liar, Jessica."

"Oh, of course not," Jessica put in hastily. "I never thought you were! And I'm sure if you explained to Janet—"

"I tried to explain," Denny said bitterly. "She wouldn't listen, remember?"

"Well, she was so hurt at the time. She couldn't hear you," Jessica said. "Give her another chance. You guys always had a great time together. Think about the picnic—it would be so much more fun, wouldn't it, if you were hanging out with Janet?" *And I wasn't?*

Denny dabbed at the corner of his eye with the napkin. "I did want to ask her when I first heard about it. But since she wasn't talking to me at the time, it was kind of hard."

"She'd definitely talk to you now," Jessica promised. *If I have anything to say about it.* "So what do you say? Can you forgive her?"

Denny shrugged and went back to eating his ice cream. "If Janet's willing to forget what happened and forgive me, then I guess I can do the same for her."

All right! Jessica thought. Now all she had to do was convince Janet to forgive Denny.

Seven

◇

"Jessica, what are *you* doing here?" Janet opened
the door to her house. She stared at Jessica with an
unfriendly look. "If you wanted to drop by, you
should have called first. We're about to sit down to
dinner."

She's as charming as ever, Jessica thought. *Why
doesn't she pull the welcome mat out from under my
feet? I don't even know why I'm trying to make her hap-
pier — she doesn't deserve it.*

Oh, yeah. I'm doing this for me, not for her, Jessica
realized.

"Sorry if I came at a bad time. But I was on my
way home, and the most unbelievable thing happened. This won't take long. Don't worry." Jessica
walked into the Howells' spacious house. She
tossed her tiny purse and her shopping bag full of

the clothes she had worn to school onto a chair in the foyer.

"So what do you want?" Janet asked, leading Jessica into the living room. "I just saw you half an hour ago. Couldn't it have waited until tomorrow?"

"Janet, look. I . . . well, I felt bad about how you left Casey's," Jessica said, glad her motivation was clear. "In a hurry and all. I was sort of worried."

"Hmpf." Janet sank onto the couch. "Don't worry about me. I'm fine."

"Right. I know. Anyway, the most amazing thing happened when I was on my way out of Casey's," Jessica went on, sitting in a rocking chair by the window. "I ran into *Denny*."

Janet's eyes widened, and for the first time all day she actually seemed happy. "Really?" she asked. Then she seemed to catch herself. "I mean, uh, too bad you had to bump into that jerk. I hope you didn't talk to him."

"Well . . . as a matter of fact, I did," Jessica said, rocking back and forth in the chair. "I mean, I couldn't help it. He talked to me first."

"Why? Did he want to tell you he was studying for a science test while he was sitting there eating an ice cream sundae?" Janet picked up a pillow and punched it a few times, as if she was imagining Denny's face on the front of it.

"Actually, Janet . . . he wanted to talk to me about *you*," Jessica said slowly.

"About me?" Janet sat up straighter on the sofa. "What about me?" She tossed her hair over her shoulder.

"He asked me if I thought you'd go to the picnic with him," Jessica said.

"Yeah, right," Janet scoffed.

"He did!" Jessica insisted.

Janet put the pillow down and stared at her. "Seriously?"

Jessica nodded. "Yes. He asked me to find out if you'd consider being his date."

"Consider it? Sure, I'll consider anything. But I'm not going with him," Janet declared.

"Aren't you even going to think it over?" Jessica asked.

Janet shrugged. "Why should I?"

"Because he's really, really upset. And he's trying to make things up to you. Don't you see?" Jessica asked.

"He's going to have to try a little harder than that. I want an apology—in person," Janet said. "Sending you over as his little messenger doesn't count."

"But Janet, he's devastated!" Jessica said.

Janet raised an eyebrow. "Devastated? Jessica, come on."

"He *was*," Jessica insisted. She could tell that

Janet wasn't going to believe her unless she made the story really good. And the only way to do that was to embellish the truth. *Just a little. OK, a lot.*

"Janet, he'd be really embarrassed if you knew this," Jessica began. *Not to mention mad at me.* "But Denny was actually *crying.* He was wiping tears out of his eyes the whole time we talked."

"You're kidding," Janet said, a skeptical look on her face.

Jessica shook her head. "No, I'm not." OK, so it was hay fever, not Janet fever, but he had definitely dabbed at his eyes once or twice. That made what she was saying the truth—technically. "And this was right in the middle of Casey's—where anyone could see him! Even other *guys.*" She paused to let the significance of that statement sink in. "But I guess he doesn't care who knows. He's that crazy about you." She leaned back in the chair and let out a loud sigh. "True love. It's so romantic!"

"I can't believe he cares that much," Janet said in a soft voice, gazing off into the distance.

Neither can I, Jessica thought. "Believe it," she told Janet.

"In that case, maybe I should think about it." Janet tapped her fingernails against the coffee table.

Jessica watched her friend's expression closely. Janet wasn't exactly smiling. But she didn't look as if she was about to attack anyone either.

"If Denny calls me and asks me to the picnic himself," Janet finally said, "I'll go with him."

"All right!" Jessica cried. Everything was working out exactly the way she wanted it to!

Janet stared at her. "What are *you* so excited about?"

"Oh, um—you and Denny, making up. I always thought you made such a great couple," Jessica said sweetly.

"We did, didn't we," Janet mused. "Maybe we can get back together."

And if you do, Jessica thought, *you'll owe it all to me!*

"What are you so happy about?" Elizabeth asked, pausing in the doorway of her sister's bedroom. "You've been smiling and humming every time I've walked by, the whole time you've been doing your math homework. You're kind of worrying me. That's not like you."

"I'm in such a great mood, I can't help it!" Jessica pushed her chair back from her desk and put her hands behind her head. "Did you ever have one of those days where everything, absolutely everything, went right?"

"Sure," Elizabeth said with a smile. "Why? Is that what happened to you today?"

Jessica nodded. "Actually, it wasn't so much that it happened. It's that I *made* it happen."

"You mean . . . getting a B on the math test so you could buy those new clothes?" Elizabeth was puzzled. She sat on Jessica's bed and waited for her to explain. Knowing her twin, this could take a while—she might as well get comfortable.

"That was just part of it," Jessica said. She scooted her chair over to the bed. "Don't tell Mom and Dad. But I really didn't get a B on that test."

"You didn't? Are you saying you changed the grade?" Elizabeth asked. "Jessica, that's terrible!"

Jessica shook her head. "No, I didn't—Mr. Glennon changed the grade. He let me do an extra-credit project this afternoon. I walked his dog, told him how many meters it was from his house to the park, and measured some other stuff, and *then* he gave me a B."

"That was pretty nice of him," Elizabeth said.

"I thought so too," Jessica agreed. "Especially since it got me the money I needed to buy a new dress. And *that* got me two dates to the picnic."

"Two dates? Wow, I'm impressed." Elizabeth grinned at her twin. "That must be some dress. So who asked you?"

"Bruce and Aaron," Jessica said.

"Oh. Well, at least you didn't have to spend much time choosing which guy to go with," Elizabeth said. "You picked Aaron, right?"

"No," Jessica said, smiling.

Elizabeth couldn't believe her ears. Since when did Jessica prefer Bruce to Aaron? "You picked Bruce Patman over Aaron?"

"Nope!" Jessica said.

"You mean . . . you turned them *both* down? Why? Who do you want to go with?" Elizabeth asked. "Mike McCluskey?"

"No. I'm keeping both dates," Jessica said. "I'm going to the picnic with Bruce *and* with Aaron."

"What? But you can't do that," Elizabeth said. "They'll never go for that."

"Sure I can do it," Jessica said, "because they won't know. I'll have one of them pick me up at home. I'll tell the other that I'll meet him there. I can set up two picnic blankets—one with Aaron, and one with Bruce—in two different locations."

"That's horrible," Elizabeth said. "They'll be furious when they find out!"

"But Elizabeth, they *won't* find out," Jessica said confidently. "I know I can make them both think they're my one and only date."

Elizabeth frowned. "I still say you're being really dishonest to both of them."

"It's not my fault they both asked me," Jessica said.

"No, but it's your fault you accepted both dates," Elizabeth told her. "Is that what you meant by your day going so perfectly?"

"No, that was only part of it. The best part of it is that I managed to get Denny and Janet to think they want to get back together. So I won't have to go to the picnic with Janet, because she'll go with Denny," Jessica explained.

"Now I'm really confused," Elizabeth said, frowning.

Jessica quickly told her about the situation with Janet and how she'd demanded an escort to the picnic. "So Lila got a date with Mike before I got a date—which means I'd have to go with Janet. She won't go with any boy besides Denny. So I decided to get Denny and Janet back together."

Elizabeth frowned. "And how did you do that?"

"I told Denny that Janet said she was sorry, and I told Janet that Denny said the same thing," Jessica announced proudly.

"And did they say that?" Elizabeth asked.

"Not in so many words, but—"

"So you *lied* to them?" Elizabeth cried. "I can't believe you, Jessica. You spent the whole day lying! Is that what you call a perfect day?"

"Well, yeah," Jessica admitted with a shrug.

"When it all works out as well as it did, who cares about a couple of little white lies? They don't hurt anybody. I had to lie. Anybody else would have done the same thing."

"No, they wouldn't," Elizabeth replied, rolling her eyes.

"Yes, they would have. Everybody lies, Elizabeth. Grow up," Jessica said.

"Growing up has nothing to do with lying. I don't tell lies. And I'm never going to," Elizabeth declared.

"Oh, come on, Elizabeth. I've *heard* you lie," Jessica told her confidently. "Don't give me that."

"No, I don't lie," Elizabeth protested. "I don't believe in lying!"

"You're lying right now!" Jessica yelled. "I know you've lied in the past. We've told lies together—to get out of trouble. I know it, and you know it!"

Elizabeth stood up, her face growing hot with anger. "If I ever did lie, I'm sure I was only doing it to cover for you!" she cried. "And you know what? I'm never going to lie for you again!"

"I don't need you to!" Jessica yelled.

"I know. You can tell a million lies on your own, without anyone's help—you've proved that!" Elizabeth retorted. "Well, have fun, but count me out from now on. You can be a liar if you want, but I'm not!"

"You think you're so right all the time," Jessica said as Elizabeth stormed out the door. "You don't know the first thing about lying!"

"And I don't want to!" Elizabeth shot back, slamming the door behind her.

Jessica folded back the comforter on her bed. She knew she should go to sleep soon, but she was still upset about her argument with Elizabeth. She couldn't stop pacing around her bedroom.

What was so terrible about lying? When it didn't hurt anyone and it helped things move along faster than normal, what was the big deal about telling a couple of lies? A person couldn't be honest one hundred percent of the time. If Elizabeth thought she could be, then she was already telling a lie—to herself. At least Jessica was truthful about her lying. She didn't pretend that she was above it.

Jessica paused beside her bedroom window and gazed out at the night sky. Dozens of stars sparkled in the darkness. Jessica searched for a constellation, but she couldn't find one.

Why couldn't Elizabeth take her side, just once? Why did she always have to do the direct opposite of whatever Jessica did?

Elizabeth's words echoed in her head. *I don't tell lies. And I'm never going to. I don't believe in lying.* Did she have to act so superior about it? Couldn't she see that once in a while a person *had* to lie? Telling the truth all the time just didn't work.

At just that moment a meteor streaked across the sky. *People say that if you wish on a falling star, your wish will come true,* Jessica remembered. *Well, I wish Elizabeth would see why you can't tell the truth all the time. I wish she could see that being a hundred percent honest isn't all it's cracked up to be!*

Eight

"Good morning, Elizabeth." Mr. Bowman stopped in the doorway of the *Sixers* office on Wednesday morning.

"Oh, hi, Mr. Bowman," Elizabeth said with a sigh, glancing up at her English teacher.

Mr. Bowman settled into a chair beside her. "How's it going?" he asked, indicating her paper.

"Rotten," Elizabeth said. Then she smiled uneasily. "Sorry. I didn't mean to bark at you like that."

"No problem. I guess you're as tired as I am," Mr. Bowman said with a chuckle.

"No, I don't think so. I don't have huge dark circles under my eyes like you do," Elizabeth said.

Mr. Bowman's eyes widened, and his eyebrows shot up.

Elizabeth clapped her hand over her mouth. "Gosh, I'm sorry. I didn't mean that."

"It's . . . all right," Mr. Bowman said slowly. He rubbed his face with the palms of his hands, as if he were still trying to wake up.

I can't help it, Elizabeth thought. *He does look exhausted. I was only being honest about it.*

"So, do I dare ask"—Mr. Bowman pointed to the computer keyboard in front of Elizabeth—"how your essay is coming along?"

Elizabeth stared at the empty computer screen in front of her. She considered telling Mr. Bowman some story about how she'd been working really hard on her essay and that it was almost done. Or she could tell him that she had writer's block—she was sure he would be sympathetic. But what was the point? She might as well tell him the truth. Honesty was the best policy, after all.

"To tell you the truth, Mr. Bowman, I haven't even started it," Elizabeth said.

"You haven't *started* it? But Elizabeth, the deadline is next week," Mr. Bowman said. "I wanted to go over your first draft today, so I could help you streamline your argument."

"I know, but . . ." Elizabeth shrugged. "What can I say? I just don't feel like writing it."

"You don't feel like writing? But you write all the time," Mr. Bowman argued.

"I think it's kind of a dumb topic," Elizabeth said. Then she clapped her hand over her mouth again. "I mean, not dumb, exactly, but—well, yeah. Really boring. Dry as toast."

"Well, Elizabeth, er, uh, do what you can with it," Mr. Bowman said, standing up, his face going slightly pale. "Sorry to bother you!" He rushed off into the hallway.

Elizabeth flicked a switch, turning off the computer. What was Mr. Bowman acting all freaked out about? Sure, she didn't usually speak her mind so freely. But that was no reason for Mr. Bowman to be so shocked.

"I think your hair looks fantastic," Jessica said as she leaned against the locker next to Lila's. It was early on Wednesday morning, just before school started for the day. So what if Lila had won their bet? Jessica wasn't about to let her win at *everything*. Lila deserved to have bad hair—in exchange for trying to outsmart Jessica and landing a date with Mike McCluskey! Even if Jessica had gotten out of going to the picnic with Janet, it was no thanks to Lila. If anything, Lila owed her.

"Then how come no one's complimented me on my perm?" Lila asked, frowning as she examined her reflection in her small handheld mirror.

"Lila, isn't it obvious? They're jealous," Jessica said, patting Lila's arm as she took the mirror away and put it back in Lila's locker. "You look so fabulous, they don't want to call any more attention to you. That's why they're not complimenting you."

Lila frowned. "Really?" She didn't sound convinced. Pressing her palms against the sides of her head, she tried to flatten her hair against her ears.

"Really. I overheard a couple of girls saying they wanted to get their hair done just like yours," Jessica promised her friend. *Of course, that was* before *you got the perm.*

"Well, that makes me feel a little better. I was starting to worry," Lila said, taking a science textbook out of her locker and stuffing it into her backpack.

"There's nothing to worry about," Jessica assured her.

Lila closed her locker, and she and Jessica started walking down the hall toward homeroom.

As they passed Elizabeth's locker Lila suddenly stopped. "I want a second opinion," she announced, and Elizabeth looked up.

"No problem," Jessica said with a shrug. "Elizabeth doesn't know that much about hair, but—"

"That's OK. I want to know what the average person thinks," Lila said.

"What did you want a second opinion about?" Elizabeth asked. "And since when am I average? If anything, I think I'm above average. In fact, if you look at the charts—"

"Chill out! I didn't mean anything bad by it," Lila said. "It's just that you don't know me as well as Jessica, so your opinion could be more ob . . . ob . . ."

"Objective," Elizabeth said. "I think that's the word you're looking for. I'll try anyway. What's this about?"

"My hair," Lila said. "What do *you* think of my new perm, Elizabeth?"

Jessica smiled. *OK, Ms. I Shall Not Tell a Lie*, she thought. *Let's see how you handle this.* Jessica watched her twin as she considered Lila's hairstyle from every angle. Her forehead was creased with concentration.

Oh, give it up, Elizabeth, Jessica thought. *You know good and well that you're going to say something nice, no matter how bad it is.* The night before, she'd wished that Elizabeth would realize that a person couldn't tell the truth all the time. This was the perfect opportunity! Elizabeth was sure to understand that this was a situation that required lying. Not much, of course—just a little white lie so that she wouldn't hurt Lila's feelings.

"Well?" Lila prompted. "Come on, Elizabeth. Tell me what you really think."

"I don't know how to say this, Lila. But your perm really looks terrible," Elizabeth finally told her. "It's just awful."

Jessica's jaw nearly dropped to the floor. What did Elizabeth think she was doing?

"Wh-What?" Lila asked.

"It's atrocious. Your hair looked much better before you got that perm," Elizabeth said. Then she chewed her thumbnail, looking uneasy. "I'm sorry. Was that too blunt? I didn't mean for it to come out like that."

"You couldn't get any blunter!" Jessica said.

"I asked her for the truth," Lila said, her jaw clenched.

Elizabeth nodded. "Well, the truth is important. And since you asked, I'd recommend getting your hair fixed—immediately. In fact, maybe you should take today off and head straight for the beauty salon," she suggested.

Jessica gasped. "Cut it out, Elizabeth! Are you trying to be mean on purpose?"

"No, I'm *not* trying to be mean," Elizabeth said. "And I'm really sorry, Lila. But there's no point lying now. Not when you've got a disaster on your hands—I mean, head."

"Well." Lila's face began to turn red. She tried to toss her hair, but the curly mass barely moved.

"That's just your opinion. Your hair isn't great either, if you want to know the truth—"

"But Lila, this isn't just my opinion." Elizabeth shook her head. "Everyone has been calling you Octopus Head ever since you got that perm." She put her hand on Lila's arm in sympathy. "I don't want to tell you this, but I feel like I have to. Lila, everyone's been laughing at you behind your back."

"No! But—but—this is horrible!" Lila turned to Jessica. "Did you know about this?"

Jessica tried her best to look shocked and outraged. "Me? Of course n—"

"Yes," Elizabeth cut her off. "She did. Look, Jessica, I'm sorry, but it's true, and I can't hold back the truth any longer! I told Jessica to tell you, Lila, but she wouldn't."

"You . . . I hate you!" Lila shouted at Jessica, angry tears streaming down her cheeks. "You lied to me! I wanted to get it fixed right away, but you talked me out of it. Only so you could make me look like an idiot!"

"Lila, I can explain—" Jessica said.

"No, you can't! Don't bother trying!" Lila took off, running down the hall at top speed.

"Lila, wait! Lila!" Jessica cried, dashing after her. She felt absolutely awful. She had never expected Lila to be so upset. Jessica chased Lila down the first-floor hallways, skidding as she rounded a corner. There was Lila, disappearing down the corridor.

"I'm sorry!" Jessica called after her. "I didn't mean to—"

"Stay away from me," Lila yelled over her shoulder. "I never want to speak to you again!"

"Dude, you won't believe this. But I actually have *two* dates for the picnic."

Elizabeth stopped on her way out of the school library. *Is that Bruce Patman's voice?*

She peeked around the door and saw Bruce standing in the hallway. *Uh-oh,* Elizabeth thought as she noticed the other boy he was standing with. *Aaron Dallas. Are Jessica's two dates having a conversation about the picnic?* This couldn't turn out well.

"Two dates, huh? How did that happen?" Aaron asked. He took a sip from the water fountain and wiped his mouth on his shirtsleeve.

"You know how irresistible I am." Bruce laughed.

Elizabeth felt her stomach turn over. Bruce was so conceited, it was revolting. And suddenly she had a nearly irresistible impulse to tell him so.

"Actually," he went on, "I asked one girl to go with me. She said yes. Naturally," Bruce bragged. "Then this *other* totally cute girl asked *me*. How was I supposed to say no to someone with such great taste?"

"So why don't you just break the first date?" Aaron asked. "Like most people would?"

"Because I don't want to," Bruce said. "Anyway, what guy wouldn't want two cute dates?"

"I wouldn't," Aaron said. "And even if I did want two dates, I'd be too nervous about how I was going to pull it off. There's no way."

"It'll be easy." Bruce laughed. "I'll just set up one picnic blanket at the front of the park, and another at the rear. The place is going to be crowded, right? I'll just go back and forth between them. They won't see. Nobody's feelings will get hurt."

"It's still terrible," Aaron said. "Man, that's so *rude!*"

Bruce laughed. "Hey, the way I see it, half of a date with me is better than a whole date with anyone else, right?" He slapped Aaron on the back, then walked off down the hall.

Aaron was shaking his head as Elizabeth stepped out from behind the door. He glanced at her, looking embarrassed to be caught in such a stupid conversation. "Did you hear that?"

Elizabeth nodded. She felt sheepish about eavesdropping. But she hadn't been doing it on purpose . . . exactly.

"Having two dates for the same event. Have you ever heard of anything like that?" Aaron asked. "I mean, who in the world besides Bruce Patman would have the nerve to pull off something *that* devious?"

"Well . . ." Elizabeth moved toward him. "Actually, I know someone who's planning to do the exact same thing."

"You do?" Aaron pushed up the sleeves of his long-sleeved T-shirt. "Who?"

"Jessica," Elizabeth said. *Sorry, Jessica. But I just can't cover for you. It isn't fair to Aaron!* "Aaron, I hate to break this to you. But *Jessica* is one of Bruce's dates for the picnic."

"Jessica who?" Aaron asked.

Elizabeth rolled her eyes. "Jessica, my *twin*."

"She is?" Aaron looked confused. "But she can't be. Jessica said she'd go to the picnic with me."

"I know, but that was *after* she told Bruce she'd go with him." Elizabeth shook her head, feeling awful as she saw the hurt look on Aaron's face. "I guess I shouldn't have told you. But I couldn't help it."

"No, it's OK. I'm *glad* you told me," Aaron said. "At least someone around here can tell the truth!"

"Oh, and by the way, Jessica hates that shirt you're wearing," Elizabeth added. "She can't stand it."

Aaron's eyes narrowed. "Did she say that?"

"At least twice," Elizabeth said with a shrug. "Sorry."

"Don't be sorry," Aaron said. "Jessica's the one

who should apologize!" He marched off down the hallway, looking determined.

Why did I have to add that extra, insulting bit about the shirt? Elizabeth wondered, watching Aaron. *What's wrong with me today? Can't I keep* anything *to myself?*

Jessica brushed her hair, peering into the small mirror hanging on the inside of her locker door. She smiled at herself. *Too wide,* she thought. Jessica practiced until she was showing just the right amount of teeth. *Perfect. Remember that.*

Jessica usually spent the time in between classes hanging out with Lila. But now that Lila wasn't speaking to her, thanks to Elizabeth, she was on her own.

At least my hair looks good, Jessica thought, brushing the ends so that they flipped up. *Lila probably went home sick after hearing that everyone was making fun of her hair.* Jessica rolled her eyes. Lila could be so vain.

A figure came up behind Jessica, casting a shadow over the mirror. She turned around, still holding her round brush.

"Aaron!" Jessica flashed him the smile she had just been practicing.

He didn't smile back. His mouth was turned downward into an ugly frown, and his brown eyes glared at her. "I can't believe you'd do something like this," he said in an angry tone.

"Something like what?" Jessica asked. "Wait a second—is this about Lila's hair? Because I was only trying to protect her. She's my best friend and—"

"It isn't about *Lila*. It's about you and me," Aaron said.

"You and me?" Jessica's eyes lit up. "What a nice topic. We could talk about that all day!"

"Not exactly. It's about you and me—and *Bruce Patman*," Aaron seethed.

"B-Bruce?" Jessica said. "What does he have to do with anything?" she asked. She smiled her best smile and batted her eyes, trying to appear innocent.

"Gee, I don't know. Why on earth would you make a date with me, when you already had one with him?" Aaron demanded, tapping his finger against his chin. "Because you think I'm an idiot? Because you think you can get away with anything?"

"No, I don't think that," Jessica said quickly. "And I didn't want to go with him, I wanted to go with you. Only—"

"Only you decided, hey, why choose, when you can go with both of us?" Aaron said bitterly. "Well, forget it, Jessica. You're a liar. I wouldn't go to the picnic with you if you were the last girl on earth!"

"You wouldn't?" Jessica asked.

"No. And I'm glad you hate this shirt. I'll wear it every day from now on!" He turned and stormed off.

Jessica scratched her head, confused. Since when had she said anything to Aaron about that ugly rugby shirt? The only person she could remember mentioning it to was . . . Elizabeth.

Nine

◇

"Have you seen Janet anywhere?" Elizabeth asked.

"You need to talk to Janet? Since when? About what?" Lila asked. Her hair was up in a purple baseball cap; Elizabeth guessed she had borrowed it from Mandy.

"Her and Denny." Elizabeth sighed. "Lila, they're living a lie, and they don't even know it!"

"Living a lie? What in the world are you talking about?" Lila asked, adjusting the cap.

"It's Jessica," Elizabeth said. When she saw Lila scowl, she added, "Sorry to bring her name up. But she lied in order to get Janet and Denny back together. And I have to tell them."

"She *helped* them get back together, you mean," Lila corrected her. "I mean, she couldn't do it single-handedly. Not even Jessica could tell that many lies."

Elizabeth raised an eyebrow. "Actually . . ."

Lila looked Elizabeth squarely in the eye. "What did she *do?*" she asked.

"She made each of them think the other was sorry. But they weren't," Elizabeth explained. "And they're probably together right now, when deep down, they really don't care about each other at all!"

Lila wrinkled her nose. "Are you sure?"

Elizabeth nodded. "Positive. And they have to know. I have to tell them the truth!"

"Are you *kidding?*" Lila asked, her eyes growing wide. "Or are you *insane?* You must know what Janet can be like—but now you want to go and upset her by telling her that? You *can't* tell Janet the truth. She'll break up with Denny again and—"

"I'm sorry, Lila. But I have to," Elizabeth said firmly. "No matter what the consequences are!" She turned on her heel and began walking away.

Lila quickly shut her locker. "Wait! You don't understand," she said, chasing after Elizabeth. "She'll make me break my date with Mike! She'll ruin my life! She'll ruin everyone's lives!"

Elizabeth didn't even break her stride. It didn't matter what Lila said. Elizabeth didn't feel comfortable being in the same school with two people who were as deluded as Janet and Denny. She couldn't—she wouldn't—let this lie go on!

At that moment the bell rang. "Oh, no,"

Elizabeth said. "I have to go to social studies class!"

"Good!" Lila exclaimed. "Maybe then you'll forget about this crazy idea of yours!"

Elizabeth tightened her jaw. "Don't count on it."

"Something really weird happened earlier." Jessica grabbed her books off the desk and followed her twin out of social studies. "Somehow Aaron found out that I had two dates for the picnic. He's *furious*. Plus he said something about how he knows I hate his shirt."

Elizabeth was silent as they headed down the hall.

Jessica gave her a sidelong glance. "I guess Bruce told him that I was going to the picnic with him. It must have come up in conversation, and somehow they started talking about me and—" She stared at Elizabeth, who had stopped walking. "What?"

"I cannot tell a lie," Elizabeth replied. "*I* told Aaron what you did, and how you hate his shirt."

"You cannot tell a lie? Who are you, George Washington?" Jessica scoffed.

Actually, Jessica thought, *maybe George Washington has taken over Elizabeth's body.* All of a sudden Elizabeth was definitely acting more like him and less like herself. She wasn't lying about anything. In fact, her honesty was bordering on the pathological. If Elizabeth chopped down a cherry tree in the school courtyard, she'd probably hold a special all-school assembly to confess.

"I don't know what's going on with me today, Jessica. I can't explain it," Elizabeth said. "All I know is that I just have this *need* to tell the truth."

"Well, get over it!" Jessica said. All of this truth-telling was ruining Jessica's life! First Elizabeth had bluntly told Lila about her bad hairdo, and then she'd told Aaron about Jessica's date with Bruce—what next?

"Wait a second," Jessica said. "Are you doing this to teach me some kind of lesson or something? Is this because of our argument last night? Are you doing this to get revenge on me for lying?"

"Revenge? No, that's the last thing on my mind," Elizabeth said.

"I'm kind of scared to ask this, but what's the *first* thing on your mind?" Jessica demanded.

"I've got to find Denny and Janet. I've got to tell them that their getting back together is a total farce," Elizabeth declared.

Jessica's mouth went dry. "You—you what?" she whispered.

"I just don't feel right about it. I can't get it off my mind!" Elizabeth said. "I have to tell them that they're still mad at each other."

"Why do you have to do that?" Jessica said. "That doesn't even make any sense! They're not mad at each other. They're back together."

"I can't explain it, but I have to tell them the truth. I *have* to," Elizabeth repeated, "or I'm not going to be able to sleep tonight."

Just then Jessica noticed Janet and Denny walking down the hall toward her and Elizabeth!

Jessica's heart started pounding. Janet and Denny had only barely started speaking to each other again that morning—thanks to her. If she and Elizabeth ran into them now, Elizabeth would ruin everything!

"Uh, in here, Elizabeth." Jessica sort of hip-checked her sister into a classroom they were passing.

"What are you *doing?*" Elizabeth complained. She glanced over her shoulder. "There are people in here!"

A couple of eighth-graders who were waiting for the second bell eyed the twins. Elizabeth gave them a half wave. "Hi," she said.

"Shhh!" Jessica warned her. She peered through the glass on the top half of the door, waiting for Denny and Janet to go by.

"Come on, Jessica, quit fooling around. I told you—I have to talk to Denny and Janet!" Elizabeth shoved Jessica out of the way and stepped through the door into the hallway.

Janet and Denny were practically right there! Jessica grabbed Elizabeth's arm and pulled her into the library on the other side of the hallway. "I know, but can't it wait? I'm your sister, and I really need your help!" *I need you to stay away from Janet and Denny!* "Um, with a research project. We need to use the computer. The, ah, the one that connects to the Internet. Back *there*," Jessica instructed. The farther Elizabeth got from the front door, the better. Who knew when she would run out into the hall? She was out of control!

"But I can't go to the library. I have class in three minutes," Elizabeth protested.

"It's a really fast modem," Jessica assured her. "This will take two minutes, tops."

Elizabeth frowned as she stood beside Jessica at the computer. "Couldn't this wait until after school? We could do it at home, you know."

"No, I need it for my next class," Jessica said. "I told Mrs. Arnette I'd look up something, and I—" She gulped as she saw Denny and Janet walk into the library, hand in hand.

"Actually, the Internet's really slow today." Jessica jumped out of the chair. "Let's look this up in the old-fashioned encyclopedias!" She started pulling Elizabeth toward the reference section. Then she grabbed a volume off the shelf and started flipping through it, holding the heavy book in front of her and Elizabeth's faces so that they couldn't be seen.

"What *are* you looking up anyway?" Elizabeth asked.

"Uh . . . wait . . . here it is! The number of . . . potato farms in the state of Maine!" Jessica nodded knowingly. "Yup. Exactly what I told Mrs. Arnette. There are a ton of them."

Elizabeth raised her eyebrows. "How did that come up in social studies class?"

"Oh, well, you know. We had french fries for lunch yesterday. It kind of got us going," Jessica said. She snapped the book closed and looked around furtively through the library stacks. No sight of Janet anywhere. No Denny. The coast was clear!

Elizabeth shook her head as the bell for class rang. "Jessica, sometimes you're really weird."

Jessica shrugged. "What can I say?" *Except that I'm glad I managed to keep you away from Janet and Denny. Another job well done!*

Elizabeth stood beside the basketball court, waiting for a break in the game. She knew she should be working on her essay for Mr. Bowman. But she couldn't concentrate on anything until everyone knew the truth!

"Bruce!" she called out as the two boys' teams separated for a time-out. "Bruce, I need to talk to you!"

Bruce gave her a curious look, then strode toward her, wiping sweat off his forehead with a towel. "What's so important that you had to find me here?"

"It's about the picnic," Elizabeth said.

"Oh, *that*. Sorry, Elizabeth. But I already have a

date." Bruce held out his hand, examining a chipped fingernail. "You have to move a little faster than that if you want to catch Bruce Patman."

"You know, you're really a conceited jerk," Elizabeth said. Then she sucked in her breath, nervously watching Bruce's reaction. She hadn't meant to tell him the *whole* truth.

"I'm *what?*" Bruce said. "Elizabeth, that's no way to get a date with me for the picnic."

"I don't *want* a date with you. I came here to tell you that one of your dates already *has* a date," Elizabeth said. "So you should break it off with her or else you'll really look like a fool."

"What? You can't be serious," Bruce said as he rubbed the back of his neck with the towel. "Nobody would even consider double booking on me."

"Jessica would. And did," Elizabeth said. "She has a date with you and another one with Aaron. Well, she used to anyway." She shrugged. "I hope I didn't hurt your feelings. But I just thought you should know."

"I can't believe you're ratting on your own sister." Bruce looked confused. "What are you, mad at her or something?"

"No. Not at all," Elizabeth said. "I just felt you should know." *And I keep getting that feeling. It won't go away until everyone knows the truth. I have to keep looking for Denny and Janet!*

*   *   *

Jessica stood in line at the lunch counter a couple of places behind Denny and Janet. She was following them. That way, if Elizabeth came near, she would have a chance to head her sister off before she did any more damage.

"The tacos look OK," Janet said, turning to look at Denny. "Or should I get pizza?"

"Whatever you want," Denny told her.

"What are you going to have? That's what *I'll* have," Janet said.

"But *I* only want to have what *you* want to have," Denny said sweetly.

Ugh, Jessica thought. She was starting to lose her appetite. They were acting so lovey-dovey, she was beginning to regret helping them make up after all.

Just then Jessica spotted Elizabeth making her way across the cafeteria. Code red! She was headed for Denny and Janet!

Jessica cut ahead in line, pushing past Grace and Mary. "Denny! Janet! How's it *going?*" she said in an ultrafriendly tone.

"Fine," Denny told her, looking a little embarrassed. He sniffled once or twice. Jessica noticed that his eyes looked red and watery too. *His allergies must be acting up again,* she thought.

"We're great," Janet said, taking a carton of milk. "Aren't we?"

"Yeah, we're—*ah—ah—ah-choo!*" Denny sneezed.

"Oh, no. You don't have a cold, do you?" Janet asked, looking concerned.

"No. Sorry, guys. It's my allergies. They're really starting to bug me," Denny said. He grabbed a napkin out of the holder and dabbed at his eyes. "I'm sneezing all the time and my eyes keep watering. It's almost as bad as yesterday afternoon when I saw Jessica at Casey's and she told me how upset you were about our fight."

Jessica's heart sank. She was about to be in big trouble. Elizabeth hadn't even said anything yet! Her mere *presence* made the truth rear its ugly head!

"Wait a second." Janet placed a bowl of chocolate pudding on her tray. "What did you just say? How upset *I* was about our fight?" she asked Denny.

"Well, yeah." Denny looked at her, blinking his watery eyes. "Jessica told me that you felt really bad about our fight, and—"

"Jessica told you that? Just like Jessica told *me* that *you* were really upset about our fight?" Janet demanded, glaring at Jessica. "So upset that you were crying?"

"Me, upset? No way. I wasn't *crying*. I have allergies, OK? They make my eyes water. I definitely wasn't upset. Actually, I was *angry*," Denny said, "if you want to know the truth."

"I do want the truth. And I'm going to tell *you* the truth," Janet declared. "I never even wanted to get back together. I only did it because I felt sorry for you."

"Oh, yeah? Well, I only asked you to the picnic because I felt sorry for *you!*" Denny replied.

Doesn't anyone feel sorry for me? Jessica thought, feeling trapped.

"Well, I don't need a pity date. Consider yourself canceled!" Janet yelled.

"Good!" Denny said.

"Fine!" Janet replied. "And I never want to talk to *you* again!" She pointed at Jessica, her finger shaking. "You're the worst friend I've ever had!"

"And I'll never believe a word you say again! You're a rotten liar!" Denny added, holding a bowl of pudding in his palm as if he might throw it at Jessica.

Then Janet and Denny both shoved aside their trays and stormed out of the cafeteria in opposite directions.

"Wow! What was that all about?" Elizabeth asked, stopping in front of Jessica and gazing after the unhappy ex-couple.

Jessica wheeled and faced her sister. "As if you don't know!" she practically shouted. "This is all *your* fault!"

"Me? I didn't say anything!" Elizabeth protested.

"You didn't have to," Jessica said. "Just being around you makes everyone start blabbing the truth!"

"Oh, good." Elizabeth let out a deep, happy sigh. "I'm *so* relieved it's out in the open."

"What are you doing? Are you deliberately trying to ruin my life? Or is it just working out that way?" Jessica demanded.

"What do you mean? I'm only doing what I feel is right," Elizabeth said. "It's not intentional. I just woke up this morning with this *feeling*—"

"I don't want to hear about it!" Jessica held up her hand. "And that's the truth!"

"Jessica! Jessica!"

Jessica stopped on her way out of the cafeteria. What now? Hadn't she suffered enough for one lunch period? She turned toward the voice that was calling to her.

Bruce was walking over to her, crumpling a brown paper bag in his hand. He stuffed it into the trash can and then caught up with her.

"I need to talk to you about the picnic," Bruce announced.

"Sure." Jessica smiled politely at him. He was her date, after all. Her one and only date. "Did you want to make some concrete plans?"

"Yeah, actually, I did. I wanted to make plans, all right—to dump you," Bruce said.

"What?" Jessica asked, dumbfounded.

"Elizabeth told me that you scheduled two dates for the picnic," Bruce said.

Elizabeth! What has she been doing, skipping all her classes so she can tell everyone the so-called truth?

Jessica fumed inwardly. "Well, that's technically true," she told Bruce nervously. "But the first date I accepted was with you, so that's the one that really counts—"

"Forget it, Jessica. Don't count on having me as your date for the picnic. You can sit alone, for all I care," Bruce said. "Better yet, why don't you stay home? Nobody double books on Bruce Patman!"

"Oh, yeah? Well, nobody cancels on Jessica Wakefield!" Jessica declared fiercely.

"No kidding. That's funny, I think it already happened *twice* today." Bruce gave an ugly laugh.

Jessica took one last look at him, then marched out of the cafeteria, her head held high. "I never wanted to go with you anyway!" she called over her shoulder.

Jessica dug her fork into a thick square of spinach lasagna. "Could somebody pass the garlic bread?" she asked, glaring across the table at her twin. Elizabeth had a peaceful glow on her face. It was really annoying. "Please?"

"Here you go." Jessica's mother passed the basket of aromatic bread down the table.

"Thanks," Jessica said. She ripped a piece from the loaf and put it on her plate.

"Great food, Mom. The lasagna's a little dry, though," Elizabeth said.

Jessica nearly dropped her fork. Was Elizabeth

really going to stick with this truth nonsense, even after all the trouble it had created?

"Dry? You think so?" The corners of Mrs. Wakefield's mouth turned down in a frown.

Good going, Elizabeth. Way to make Mom feel great.

"Just a little." Elizabeth smiled. "I can wash it down with some milk, though. No problem." She picked up her glass and stared at it for a second. "I think we need a new dishwasher. There are water spots all over this glass."

"Is this a new game, Elizabeth? Are you playing restaurant critic?" Steven teased.

"Actually, Elizabeth's been like this all day," Jessica said. "At school she—"

"Oh, speaking of school, Jessica, I almost forgot. Mr. Glennon called you this afternoon," Elizabeth said.

"Oh?" Jessica's voice wobbled. Now what? Couldn't Elizabeth give Jessica her phone messages in private instead of at the dinner table?

"Isn't Mr. Glennon your math teacher?" Mr. Wakefield asked.

Elizabeth and Jessica both nodded.

"Why is he calling you at home, Jessica?" Mrs. Wakefield asked.

"*I* don't know, Mom. I have no idea!" Jessica said.

"Is something wrong?" her father wondered.

"I doubt it. I probably left my notebook behind in class or something dumb like that," Jessica said. "It's not important. I'm sure Elizabeth can tell me about it later." She shot Elizabeth a warning look. If Elizabeth told the truth again and ruined things for her, she wouldn't forgive her.

"Is that what he wanted, Elizabeth?" Mrs. Wakefield asked.

"Actually, Mr. Glennon wants to know if Jessica can walk his dog," Elizabeth said, ignoring Jessica's expression. "He's going out of town. He said that since you did such a good job last time, maybe you could walk Sparky again. This time he'd even pay you."

"When did you walk Mr. Glennon's dog?" Mr. Wakefield asked, looking confused. "And why didn't he pay you last time?"

Jessica glanced across the table at Elizabeth. Her twin was looking right at her—there was no use lying about it. If she didn't tell her parents the truth, Elizabeth would do it for her. Maybe they'd appreciate the truth more if they heard it straight from her lips.

"It's kind of a long story," she hedged.

"We're all ears," Mr. Wakefield replied, raising his eyebrows.

Jessica took a deep breath. There was no easy way to say this. "Remember that math test? The one you wanted me to get a B on? Well . . . I didn't

exactly get a B. But I sort of did—I mean, technically. It depends on how you look at it."

Steven gasped. "Are you saying you *didn't* get a
B? I think I'm going to faint. Water! Water!"

"Be quiet, or you'll be wearing it, not drinking it,"
Mr. Wakefield warned Steven with a stern glance.

"As you were saying?" Mrs. Wakefield prompted
Jessica.

"Well, I did get a B. But it started out as a C,"
Jessica explained.

"And it turned into a B?" Mr. Wakefield asked.
"Somehow I don't think I'm going to like this
story."

"Did you change the grade, Jessica?" Mrs.
Wakefield sounded very disappointed. "Did you
lie to us?"

"No!" Jessica cried. "I mean, I changed the
grade, but not how you think. I did a bunch of
extra-credit work. Mr. Glennon changed my grade
the same afternoon."

"After you walked his dog? That counts for
extra credit?" Mr. Wakefield asked.

"Boy, that school's gotten a lot easier since I
went there," Steven said, and Elizabeth gave a
small giggle.

Jessica frowned across the table at her. There
was nothing funny about this! "Mr. Glennon had
me measure a whole bunch of stuff at the park
using the metric system. That was the section I

didn't do well on in the test. After he saw that I knew how to do conversions, he changed my test grade to a B. So I *did* get a B," Jessica argued.

"Not really," Mr. Wakefield disagreed. "You got a C. Only your teacher needed you to walk his dog, so you weaseled your way into a B. That wasn't exactly fair."

"We told you that if you got a B on the test, we'd give you the money to buy some new clothes," Mrs. Wakefield added. "You didn't get a B. When you showed us your test without explaining, you lied to us."

"What's the difference? A B's a B," Jessica said.

Mr. Wakefield shook his head. "Not in this case, it isn't. I'm afraid we're going to have to do something about this. I'm sure there's no chance of getting the clothing money back."

Jessica shook her head. "Not really. I already wore the clothes I bought."

"But you said they were for the picnic," Mrs. Wakefield said. "Does that mean you lied to us again?"

"No! The clothes weren't *technically* for the picnic, but they were connected to the picnic, and—"

"Jessica, we've heard enough. Consider yourself grounded. *Technically*," her father said. "I want you to come home every day, immediately after school. And you won't go to any social events for a month."

A month? Jessica slumped in her chair, her appetite disappearing. The lasagna *was* dry. There *were* spots on the dishes. And the milk wasn't cold enough. But did she go around pointing out everyone's flaws?

No. That was Elizabeth's job. And if Elizabeth didn't quit being so brutally honest, Jessica would end up being grounded for life!

Jessica drummed her fingernails against the windowsill. Grounded. She wouldn't be going to the picnic with Aaron, or Bruce, or even Janet. She wouldn't be going at all.

This is all because of Elizabeth. She's been on this truth kick ever since last night, when I wished she'd learn that telling the truth all the time wouldn't work.

Instead, it seemed as if her wish had backfired. Elizabeth had woken up with a strange *feeling* that she needed to tell the truth. She couldn't be talked out of it. She was acting as though she were possessed or something. After just twenty-four hours of nonstop truth, Jessica had lost her best friends, two potential boyfriends, and her freedom. She couldn't go on like this! She had to knock Elizabeth out of whatever kind of weird trance she was in!

Jessica stared out the window at the stars above for a while, musing about her problem.

About ten minutes later she saw another meteor flash through the sky, just as one had the night before. Gazing at it, Jessica concentrated with all her might.

"Please make Elizabeth *stop* telling the truth," she whispered.

Ten

◇

Two slices of wheat bread popped up, and Jessica pulled them out of the toaster. She dropped the toast on her plate and smeared some butter over the slices. She was so tired, she could barely hold the knife.

She glanced up as her twin entered the kitchen, the heels of her sandals clicking loudly on the linoleum floor.

"Good morning!" Elizabeth said cheerfully. "Wow, toast. That smells great."

Jessica chewed slowly as her sister got a plate from the cabinet and a knife from the drawer. After all the trouble Elizabeth had gotten her into the day before, Jessica could hardly bear her sister's cheery tone. Not only had both of her dates to the picnic canceled on her, but now she was grounded. She didn't even know why she'd gotten out of bed that morning. She might as well just stay in her room until the end of the school year.

"You're awfully quiet this morning," Elizabeth said, brushing a stray strand of hair off her face. "Is everything OK?"

Jessica crunched into a piece of toast without saying a word. Obviously everything wasn't OK, but maybe Elizabeth was. Jessica was waiting for her to say something so that she could figure out whether her twin was back to normal or not.

"Oh, I know what it is." Elizabeth dropped two slices of bread into the toaster for herself. "I'm so sorry, Jessica. I was still so sleepy, I forgot that the first thing I wanted to do this morning was apologize to you."

"Huh?" Jessica asked.

"I'm really sorry about yesterday, Jessica." Elizabeth unscrewed the top of a jar of orange marmalade. "I never meant to mess things up. I guess I got carried away with telling the truth and all."

Jessica wiped her mouth with a napkin and stared at her twin. "Carried away? That's putting it mildly. You were on a crusade or something."

"I was?" Elizabeth poured herself a cup of orange juice from the pitcher on the table. "I didn't think of it that way. At least, that wasn't my plan."

"Then what *was* your plan?" Jessica asked. *And don't tell me you didn't have one,* she thought. *Because I won't believe it.*

Elizabeth shrugged. "I don't know. I didn't have one."

Jessica rolled her eyes, exasperated. "But you kept saying how you woke up with this feeling. And you couldn't rest until you told everyone the blunt truth," Jessica reminded her.

"I don't remember that," Elizabeth said. "But I do know that I sort of made things difficult for you. And starting today, I'm going to try to help get things back to where they were—before I messed them up. I'm going to fix things. I know it's not much, but—"

"No! It's great," Jessica told her with a bright smile. "Whatever you can do, I'll really appreciate it."

"Sure thing, sis!" Elizabeth promised.

Jessica was halfway to the sink with her dirty dishes when she stopped. "Sis? You never call me that."

"Well, you are my sister, right?" Elizabeth said. "I mean, that's what we are—sisters. Sisters and best friends." She smiled sweetly at Jessica.

Jessica felt goose bumps on her arms. For some reason Elizabeth's smile looked . . . phony. But why would she fake a smile for Jessica?

"You know, this is the *best* toast I've ever had."

Elizabeth wiped her mouth with a napkin. "This bread is fantastic."

"Don't you think it's a little . . . stale? Dry, maybe?" Jessica asked. The expiration date on the end of the bag was three days ago.

"No, not at all," Elizabeth said. "This tastes freshly baked!"

Jessica felt a prickle on the back of her neck. Why did she get the funny feeling that Elizabeth had changed drastically overnight?

Jessica slipped her sweater off her shoulders. Opening her locker, she started to hang her lime green cardigan on the hook in the back.

"Aaron! Do you have a minute?" She heard Elizabeth's voice coming from down the hall.

Jessica peered around her locker door and saw Aaron and Elizabeth standing a few feet away. Aaron was wearing a blue and brown striped T-shirt, jeans, and sand-colored suede sneakers. He was balancing a soccer ball in one hand while he carried his books with another.

I wish he weren't so mad at me, Jessica thought, watching him. *What was I ever thinking, telling Bruce I would go to the picnic with him?*

"Hi, Elizabeth. What's up?" Aaron asked, stopping in front of her.

Jessica gazed at Aaron wistfully as he chatted with Elizabeth. It wasn't fair that *Elizabeth* got to talk to him when she was the one who had messed everything up.

"I really need to talk to you," Elizabeth said. "It's incredibly important."

Jessica held her breath. Since when did Aaron and Elizabeth talk about anything important?

"Remember yesterday, when I told you that Jessica had two dates to the picnic?" Elizabeth asked.

Jessica stood there, open-mouthed. *I can't believe she's bringing this up again,* she thought. *Does she want to tell Aaron about something* else *I've done?*

"Yes," Aaron said coldly. "I remember."

"Well, it turns out that isn't what happened," Elizabeth said. "Not even close. I got it *all* wrong."

Jessica lost her grip on her backpack, nearly dropping it on her foot. She managed to catch it at the last second. What was Elizabeth doing, rewriting history?

Jessica busied herself at her locker, trying not to look as though she was eavesdropping.

"You got it wrong? How do you mean, Elizabeth?" Aaron asked. He sounded suspicious.

"Jessica didn't have two dates for the picnic after all," Elizabeth announced.

Yes, I did, Jessica thought.

"No, she didn't. Not at all. See, Bruce Patman did ask Jessica to the picnic. But she turned him *down,*" Elizabeth said.

"She did?" Aaron asked.

I did? Jessica wondered. *What's Elizabeth talking about?*

"Yes. She told him that she couldn't go with him," Elizabeth went on. "But you know Bruce. He's so conceited that he didn't even *listen* to her answer. He just assumed she'd say yes, so that's what he heard. As far as Jessica knew, when she told you yes, that was the only date she had. Of course she'd only want to go with you!" Elizabeth erupted into a fake-sounding laugh. Jessica couldn't believe what she was hearing.

"I don't know, Elizabeth. That's kind of hard to believe," Aaron said.

I agree! Especially since it didn't happen that way, Jessica thought, biting her fingernails.

"Jessica didn't ask you to say this for her, did she?" Aaron asked.

"No! It's the truth. Honest," Elizabeth said. "I mean, doesn't it *sound* like something Bruce would do? Not even listen and just assume every girl wants to go out with him?"

Aaron chuckled. "Yeah, it does kind of sound like Bruce. I'll give you that."

"So Jessica really didn't double-book," Elizabeth said. "I know you were mad at her, but do you think you could forgive her now that you know the truth?"

Truth? But you're flat-out lying! Jessica closed

her locker door, a shiver going down her spine. Before she'd gone to sleep, she'd wished that Elizabeth would stop telling the truth all the time. But now her twin had turned into a compulsive liar! Jessica didn't know why, but the idea of Elizabeth lying was very upsetting. It wasn't natural!

She hurried off down the hall in the opposite direction, hiding from Elizabeth and Aaron. She knew she should be glad that Elizabeth had smoothed things over with Aaron . . . and she was. Kind of.

But she was also kind of afraid of what would happen next. Would Elizabeth publish a new *Sixers* edition full of made-up stories? Would she tell the principal, Mr. Clark, that his bald head looked beautiful? Even worse, would she keep calling Jessica "sis"?

"Mr. Bowman! I'm so glad I found you." Elizabeth rushed into the *Sixers* office and dropped her books on a desk.

"You are?" Mr. Bowman asked, looking up from his desk. The current edition of the student newspaper was spread out on top. "I was just doing some proofreading."

"That's great. I came by because I realize I might have been kind of, um, *abrupt* yesterday," Elizabeth said. "And maybe I wasn't very nice to talk to or anything."

"Well, er . . ."

"It's OK, Mr. Bowman! I was just in this really weird mood. I can't explain. Sort of like a trance, actually," Elizabeth said. She felt as though she'd just gotten rid of a really nasty flu. Now she could breathe again!

Only it wasn't quite as easy as that. Because she'd made so many mistakes the day before, she was going to have do some scheming to get herself out of trouble.

"I'm kind of afraid to ask, but does this good mood have anything to do with your essay? Did you work through your writer's block?" Mr. Bowman asked.

"Oh, yeah." Elizabeth waved her hand in the air. "No problem."

"I thought you said the topic was boring," Mr. Bowman said.

"Boring? Goodness gracious, no. It's a *thrilling* topic," Elizabeth said. "I could write about it for pages and pages. And I *did*, last night."

"You did?" Mr. Bowman asked.

"Sure!" Elizabeth said, and flashed a bright smile. *Well, I wrote it in my head anyway*, she reasoned. *I mean, I thought about it while I was falling asleep. But I didn't exactly get out of bed and write anything on paper.*

"So, could I see it?" Mr. Bowman asked.

"You could definitely see it," Elizabeth said. *If it*

existed. Which it doesn't. "Only . . . there's a small problem."

"Computer glitch?" Mr. Bowman suggested.

"*Puppy* glitch," Elizabeth said. "My parents gave me and Jessica this adorable puppy. For our birthday."

"But I thought you had a summer birthday," Mr. Bowman said, his forehead creased.

"Oh, see, actually, this was for *last* year's birthday. But we kept waiting because we wanted the perfect puppy," Elizabeth said. *Mr. Bowman thinks I'm good at writing stories. He should appreciate this one!* "So we found out about this litter of puppies in Los Angeles. And we drove down there to get the puppy when he was old enough. But he's really homesick. And every time he sees something about Los Angeles, he totally freaks out," Elizabeth explained. "And he starts chewing anything in sight. Last night we were watching this movie called *Los Angeles Lunar Disaster*. And I guess he must have seen something on TV that reminded him of home—in fact, I think they actually showed his house—and, well, good-bye, paper. He chewed it to bits. And I wrote it in longhand, so I didn't have another copy. Sorry."

Mr. Bowman frowned. "If you didn't get the essay done, Elizabeth, you can just say so."

"But I did write it!" Elizabeth said. "And I'll

re-create it just as soon as I get a chance. Well, have a great day, Mr. Bowman. By the way, you look terrific. I *love* that striped tie with those plaid pants." She gave Mr. Bowman a thumbs-up.

"Yeah," Mr. Bowman muttered, "whatever."

"Where's Lila?" Jessica put her lunch tray down next to Mary Wallace's and sat down beside her.

"She had something to do. Not that it's any of your business." Janet glared at Jessica.

Jessica poked at the macaroni and cheese on her plate. It had been hot a few seconds ago. But the atmosphere at the Unicorner was so cold, Jessica wouldn't have been surprised if her meal suddenly became flash-frozen.

Janet was still furious at Jessica for fooling her into making up with Denny. Lila was so mad about her hair, she wasn't even eating lunch with Jessica anymore. Jessica looked around the table. Did anyone still like her, or should she eat somewhere else?

"It's funny. I always thought this table was reserved for *friends*." Janet chewed on a carrot as she cast a disapproving look at Jessica.

"Come on, Janet," Mandy said. "Jessica was only trying to help—"

Janet held up one hand, silencing her. "Spare me, OK? Jessica never does anything if it isn't in her own best interest. She doesn't care about anyone but herself."

"That's not true," Mary said. "She's always—"

"She's always *proved* that," Janet declared. "Is that what you were going to say, Mary?"

Jessica chewed glumly on a piece of macaroni. When she tried to swallow, it stuck in her throat.

"Oh, great. Like *one* Wakefield at this table wasn't enough." Janet arched one eyebrow as she stared at Elizabeth approaching the Unicorner.

Don't come over here, Jessica thought, trying to send a mental message to her sister. *If you know what's good for you, you'll stay away from Janet!*

"Janet? Can I talk to you for a second?" Elizabeth asked. "Wow. Great shirt, by the way," she added with a winning smile.

Janet frowned. "Um—thanks. So what do you want? And make it fast. I have better things to do with my lunch period."

"I want to talk to you about Jessica. Who else?" Elizabeth waved at Jessica. "Hey, sis. Enjoying lunch?"

Oh, no. She's turned into this bright, bubbly nightmare. "Yeah. It's absolutely delicious," Jessica said in a monotone.

"I'm *so* glad to hear that." Elizabeth beamed at her, then pulled up a chair beside Janet as if that were the most natural thing in the world for her to do. "OK, so here's the reason I came over. I know you're mad at Jessica. But you shouldn't be."

"Oh, *really*." Janet rolled her eyes. "And why is that?"

"Because she's your best friend. And you don't even realize it," Elizabeth said. "She's done so many things for you—"

"That's the problem," Janet interrupted.

"Good things!" Elizabeth insisted. "She's always putting *you* first. Janet, you have no idea how much Jessica looks up to you!"

Everyone at the table stared at Elizabeth, then turned and looked at Jessica, then swiveled back to Elizabeth.

I know, Jessica thought. *I don't buy it either!*

"Somehow I'm not getting this," Janet said. "Explain."

Elizabeth shook her head. "She thinks of you as her best friend, Janet. She really, really wanted to hang out with you at the picnic—more than anything. And that's because Jessica thinks you're the most amazing person at Sweet Valley Middle School."

Jessica stared at her twin in horror. Was Elizabeth out of her *mind*? She was making Jessica sound like Janet's pathetic tagalong little sister!

"But the more Jessica talked to you, the more she realized *you* wanted to spend time at the picnic with Denny," Elizabeth continued. "So she shoved her own feelings aside and tried to reunite you and Denny, even though she didn't want to go to the picnic with anyone but you. Since you're such a good friend to her."

You said that already, Jessica thought, glaring at her twin. *Cut it out!*

Janet glanced down the table at Jessica, who smiled feebly, feeling helpless. Janet's expression softened a bit and the crease in her forehead disappeared as her frown gave way to a small smile. "Wow, Jessica. Is that true?" she asked.

Jessica shrugged. She didn't know what to say. What *could* she say? She might come up with a different version than what Elizabeth already had planned for her!

"It *is* true. *So* true," Elizabeth insisted. "Please, Janet, whatever you do, don't be mad at Jessica. She only wants what's best for you. And she doesn't care if that means trampling on her own feelings. So give her another chance." Elizabeth stood up and walked over to Jessica, putting her hand on Jessica's shoulder. "I think she deserves it. Don't you?" She squeezed Jessica's shoulder. "Bye, sis. Have a great day!"

"Thanks," Jessica said. *For nothing.*

"You know, I think I'm getting along much better with Elizabeth lately," Janet mused.

Yeah—because she's gone insane! Jessica thought, watching her sister stop to chat with one of the cafeteria cooks. *She's probably telling him how wonderful the macaroni and cheese is and how they should never change the recipe.* She poked at the congealed mass of orange macaroni on her plate.

"Look out, Jessica." Mary nudged Jessica's knee under the table. "Here comes Aaron."

Jessica looked up just as Aaron stopped beside the table. "Hi, Jessica."

"Hi!" she said. *Maybe he's here to ask me to the picnic!*

"Hey, I was talking to Elizabeth this morning. And I found out I made a big mistake about the picnic. So I came over to ask—do you still want to go together?" Aaron looked nervously into Jessica's eyes. "Because I do if you do."

He was acting so romantic, right in front of everyone, that Jessica felt a little overwhelmed. She stared into his deep brown eyes. "Of course I—"

"I'm sorry, Aaron," Janet interrupted, getting to her feet. "But Jessica and I have decided to go to the picnic together."

Aaron's eyes widened. "You have?"

Jessica whirled around to look at Janet. "We have?"

"We decided that friends are more important than boys sometimes. And best friends need to stick together." Janet walked over and wrapped her arm around Jessica's shoulders.

Elizabeth, I'm going to kill you, Jessica thought.

"Oh. I didn't know," Aaron said. "Elizabeth didn't say you had a previous commitment."

"Well, she does. And we're going to have a great time at the picnic together," Janet declared. "Right, Jessica?"

"Right," Jessica mumbled, casting a forlorn look at Aaron. *Somebody rescue me. Please!*

Elizabeth walked up to Lila, who was standing by the front doors of the school. She was staring out at the cloudy sky, wearing a forlorn expression. Other kids were milling around her, unconcerned.

"What's wrong, Lila?" Elizabeth asked.

"Oh." Lila let out a loud sigh. "Nothing, really."

"Nothing?" Elizabeth said. "But you look so down. Do you have to stay after school for detention or something?" The last bell had just rung, and everyone was eager to get home.

"No. Nothing like that," Lila said.

"Well, is it about what I told you earlier?" Elizabeth asked. "That Jessica was only hiding the truth about your hair because she was jealous? Because she'd give anything to have a perm as beautiful as yours?" Elizabeth tried to hide the little smile that threatened to peek out. Her lie to Lila had been so convincing, even Elizabeth had practically believed it.

"No, not exactly. But it's sort of connected. I mean, did you ever come up with the perfect plan and then have no way of carrying it out?"

Lila asked. "No, probably not. You don't come up with complicated plans. Not like mine anyway."

"Oh, *please*. I've been working on plans all day!" Elizabeth said with a wave of her hand. "You think you're the *only* one who can do stuff like that?"

Lila turned to her, a smile curling the corners of her mouth. "Seriously?"

"As serious as telling Mr. Bowman the dog ate my homework," Elizabeth said.

"But you don't have a dog," Lila said.

Elizabeth put her hands on her hips. "I rest my case. So, are you going to let me help you or not? I'd really love to. You know how bad I feel about criticizing your hair yesterday. And I know we haven't always been close, Lila. But I love you like a sister. I really do."

"You do?" Lila asked. "Since when?"

"Since you became Jessica's best friend," Elizabeth said. She put her arm around Lila's shoulder. "Come on. Tell me what I can do."

"Well . . . OK. I have this idea. And it's funny you should mention Jessica, because it involves a big surprise for her," Lila explained.

"Jessica loves surprises!" Elizabeth cried. *Great! Now she'll know how hard I worked to get her out of trouble.* "She'll be so happy."

"I need her to come with me after school," Lila

said. "But I know she's grounded." She looked up at Elizabeth with a sweet expression. "Do you think there's *any* way you could get her out of being grounded?"

Elizabeth grinned. "Today I don't think there's anything I *can't* do."

Eleven

◇

Jessica pushed open the heavy exit door and raced out of the school building. She couldn't wait to get out of there! She was going straight to her bedroom, and she wasn't coming out—not until she could wish on another falling star. She had to make another wish—that Elizabeth would move far, far away and never interfere in her life again!

Elizabeth had stopped telling the truth, all right. She was telling nothing but *lies*. And each one of them was making Jessica's life even more unbearable!

But what if I don't see another falling star tonight—or even for weeks, maybe months? I wonder if I could wish on the sun, Jessica thought, glancing up at the sky as she started walking home. *It's a star, right? It's not falling or anything, but it might work.*

But all she could see were ominous dark gray clouds. She'd be lucky if the sky cleared that night. The way it looked now, she wouldn't be able to see any stars at all.

There was a rumble of thunder, and Jessica shivered as a stiff breeze blew at her back. Seconds later the skies above opened up and rain poured down, splattering Jessica's face.

"Aagh!" she cried, starting to run. She was still a good ten minutes from her house. She'd be drenched by the time she got home.

Who cares? Jessica thought, holding her knapsack over her head. *It's not like I'm going anywhere. Ever again!*

She jogged along the sidewalk. Her sneakers squished as she ran.

A car's horn blasted her out of her misery. Jessica turned to see a long black limousine cruising along slowly beside her. The back window rolled down smoothly.

"Jessica! Hop in!" Lila peered out, obviously trying not to get wet.

Jessica stopped running and stared at her friend as water coursed down her cheeks. "Lila?"

"Of course it's me," Lila said. "Who else in town has a limo? Hurry up and get in before you catch pneumonia."

Jessica ran over to the limousine as it slowed to a stop. "But I thought you were mad at me," she said. *And I'm afraid to ask what Elizabeth told you that made you un-mad at me.*

"I decided to forgive you," Lila said. She opened the door and scooted over on the seat. "But if you get the leather seat all wet, I don't know if Daddy will." She rummaged under the cushion and pulled out a plaid blanket. "Here, sit on this and wrap the rest of it around you so you can dry off."

"Thanks," Jessica said, stepping into the limousine. She closed the door behind her, and the driver pulled back into traffic. "You saved my life."

"Five more minutes out there and you would have melted," Lila teased. "I'm glad I saw you."

"So am I," Jessica said. "Thanks a million for the ride home."

"You're welcome. But we're not going to your house," Lila said. "Not yet."

"Oh?" Jessica asked. "Are we getting a snack on the way home?"

"Nope." Lila grinned. "Elizabeth explained the whole thing to me—what happened with my hair and why you said what you said about it."

"She did?" Jessica asked. *If she told you about my plan to keep Bruce away from you, then why do you still like me?*

Then Jessica remembered that Elizabeth wouldn't

have told Lila the *real* reason Jessica had lied about Lila's hairdo. No doubt she'd come up with another winning story to get Jessica out of trouble. Well, maybe this wasn't all bad . . . after all, she was riding in a limousine, and five minutes earlier she'd been as wet as a glass of water.

"Yes, Elizabeth explained *everything*. And I'm not mad at you anymore. In fact, *I'm* the one who should apologize to *you*," Lila continued. "That's why I decided to find you after school. I have a big surprise for you."

"You do?" Jessica asked. *Maybe I like Elizabeth the liar more than I originally thought.* Knowing Lila, the surprise was sure to be something amazing.

"Guess where we're going," Lila said. She gave Jessica a playful poke. "Just guess."

"I don't know. I can't guess," Jessica said. "Give me a hint!"

"What's the one thing you've always wanted to do but couldn't afford?" Lila asked.

Jessica bit her lip. "Could you narrow down the category a little?"

Lila laughed. "OK, I'll tell you. We're on our way to Glam! You know, that new hair and makeup place? The one that those supermodels from Los Angeles opened a couple of months ago?"

Jessica sat up, her eyes growing huge. "No

way!" She'd been wanting to check out Glam! ever since the shop had opened, but it was much too expensive for her limited budget.

"Yes way," Lila replied with a grin. "We have appointments for two-hour-long *complete* beauty makeovers. That includes everything: color consultation, manicure, shampoo and cut and style. We'll look like two new people when we're done."

"Wow." Jessica sighed, leaning back in her seat. "It's a dream come true." She pictured herself with her golden-blond highlighted hair blowing in the wind, her face covered with subtle makeup, her feet in sandals that showed off her painted toenails.

Then another picture came into focus: her mother and father waiting at the dinner table with huge frowns on their faces, telling her they'd extended her grounding into the next millennium.

"Lila, that sounds awesome. But I can't go," Jessica said. "I'm grounded. I have to go right home after school every day."

"No, you don't," Lila said. "It's OK. When I ran into Elizabeth, she said she'd tell your parents that you had to stay after school to work on a project. She's going to smooth the whole thing over for you. No worries."

Jessica smiled, staring out at the pouring rain.

No worries. Lila's right. Maybe this thing with Elizabeth and lying wasn't so bad after all. Maybe she wouldn't wish to change it that night after all!

"You are going to love this. You are going to look like a totally new person." Sergio, the stylist who'd been working on Jessica's new image, circled her chair. He pressed the towel wrapped around Jessica's head. "We are nearly done here. Just a few more seconds."

"Can I look?" Jessica asked.

"Not yet. The secret to imagining a whole new you is to miss the before and after part. Pretend that you have just been born!" Sergio exclaimed.

"Um," Jessica said, "OK."

Sergio laughed. "You will be like a baby. But not a regular little roly-poly baby. A beautiful baby. A *star* baby."

Jessica fidgeted nervously in the chair. During her entire makeover, Sergio hadn't let her see herself once. He'd polished her skin, painted her nails, and applied lipstick and some light eye makeup. Then he'd spent nearly an hour washing her hair and setting it. Now he was giving her one final minute of Absorb-a-Therapy, letting her hair drink in what he called "vital nutrients."

"Your hair will be so glossy, so shiny," Sergio said. "Like a horse's."

Jessica looked up at him. "A horse's?"

"Not a regular farm horse. A beautiful horse. A champion horse. A *star* horse," Sergio said.

Jessica liked horses as much as the next person, but she wasn't sure she wanted to look like one. Still, it was better than looking like some other animals she could think of. A hippopotamus, for example.

"Trust me," Sergio said. "The new Jessica will forget the old Jessica ever existed. You and Lila will be the most-noticed girls at this picnic. But don't forget to bring umbrellas. Rain can ruin a girl's style faster than a poorly planned low-budget layout in a fashion magazine."

"Right," Jessica said. *Whatever. Just show me how gorgeous I look, already!*

"I think we'll have a giant tent, actually," Lila said. She walked out from the back room, where another stylist, Gianni, had been working with her look. She had a big white towel wrapped around her head too.

"Well, Sergio?" Gianni said. "Is it the moment of truth?"

A timer dinged on the rolling table beside Jessica's chair. "I believe it is," Sergio said. "The hair can absorb no more! Our work here is done, Gianni."

Jessica felt a flutter of excitement in her stomach as Sergio walked over to her. She was going to look

so beautiful, she'd get *ten* dates to the picnic. And
nobody would mind sharing her either!

"*Un, deux, trois . . .*" Sergio and Gianni pulled at
the towel ends, unwrapping them at the same moment. "*Voilà!*" both stylists cried at once.

At first Jessica didn't understand what it was
that she was seeing. Then it sank in. She'd been re-
born, all right—with a perm as bad as Lila's!

"Isn't it cool?" Lila asked. "Isn't that just what
you always wanted? I hope you don't mind, but I
took the liberty of giving Sergio a small hint. I told
him which direction to take your hair in," she
added.

Jessica's stared at the floppy mass of curls falling
from her head. "Which direction was that?" she
muttered. "Down Ugly Street?" She turned to look
for Sergio, but he and Gianni had conveniently left
the girls to work on two new clients.

"Elizabeth told me that you really *did* like my
hair—so much so that you even wanted to get it
permed the same way. Only you couldn't afford it,"
Lila explained.

*You're right, I can't afford it. Not if I want to hold
my head up in public!* Jessica thought, frozen in
place. She couldn't move. She wouldn't move. She
wasn't leaving the salon!

"So this is my present to you, for sticking up for
me in front of all those kids at school who wouldn't
know style if it hit them on the head!" Lila said.

Jessica couldn't believe it. She was an Octopus Head too. No, she was *worse* than an Octopus Head. She was actually *copying* an Octopus Head. "Lila, look. It's cute to have matching hairstyles and all," Jessica began. "I'm flattered. And I really enjoyed the makeover. But we can't have the same perm!"

"We don't," Lila said in a calm voice. "Don't worry—I got mine taken out!"

Jessica spun around in her chair, facing Lila. Lila's hair was absolutely straight. It had never been straighter or more unpermed. "But you said— you—" she sputtered.

"I'm not important here. You are," Lila said. "Elizabeth made me realize that you were just jealous of my hair. So I told Sergio to make your hair extra special, and I told Gianni to turn mine back into its old, normal, boring self." She leaned over, letting her hair fall over her face. Then she stood up and it fanned around her shoulders, shiny and beautiful.

Her hair does look as good as a horse's, Jessica thought glumly. *And mine looks like a woolly mammoth's!*

"So, Jessica. What do you think of my surprise?" Lila reached out and pulled on one of Jessica's ringlet curls.

Jessica smiled uneasily. She felt like grabbing Lila's arm and wrestling her to the floor. "It's surprising, all right," she said with a sigh. *Surprisingly bad!*

*   *   *

Jessica sat at her desk, dizzy from counting the raindrops that were rolling down her window. Although she'd been trying since right after dinner, she hadn't been able to get any homework done. It was bad enough that she'd had to tell her parents that her after-school science experiment involved getting a perm. They hadn't believed her—until Elizabeth piped up and insisted that it was true. She'd said that they were studying a section on chemical interactions; half the class had perms and half the class didn't.

If that were true, I'd give anything to be in the other half, Jessica thought, pulling at her hair. *The control group.*

But it wasn't true. None of this was true, but somehow it was all real! Her hair really did look like a blond mop, thanks to Elizabeth's "helpful" lie about her envy of Lila's perm. Sure, in one way the lie had gotten her out of hot water. It was great not to have Lila hating her. But it was horrible to have a hideous hairdo!

Oh, well, Jessica thought, *it doesn't matter anyway.* This was the first time in her life that she had ever been *glad* to be grounded.

Jessica sighed. There weren't any lies that could get her out of this situation. And even if there were, she didn't want Elizabeth to think of them. She hated having a sister who was a liar, especially one who was so *bad* at it. She was totally unreliable! Unpredictable! Annoying!

Jessica put her chin in her hands and listened to another crack of thunder. If the stupid rain didn't stop soon, she'd never see a falling star. She wouldn't be able to unwish her wish of the night before. She'd be stuck with Elizabeth's lies for another day . . . maybe for the rest of her life!

A bolt of lightning lit up the night sky. Jessica jumped in fright, but not before she spotted a small dog running frantically up her street. His short white fur was drenched, and there was a terrified look in his eyes.

"Sparky!" Jessica cried, leaping out of her chair. "It's Sparky!"

Twelve

◇

Jessica yanked her plastic rain jacket off the hook at the back of the coat closet. Quickly slipping it on, she dashed out the front door and down the sidewalk. The jacket's hood kept bouncing off as she ran, causing rain to pour onto her head. Raindrops splattered against her face and got into her eyes, making it hard to see where she was going.

"Sparky!" she yelled, cupping her hands around her mouth. "Sparky, come here!" She whistled.

A crack of thunder boomed in reply, so loud that Jessica thought the sky might crack open. She cringed, pulling the jacket tighter around her.

"Sparky!" Jessica cried. "Come on, Sparky—it's OK! You're not lost, I'm right here!"

Why would Mr. Glennon let Sparky out? The little

dog was obviously scared to death of thunderstorms, Jessica thought.

Another flash of lightning burst across the sky. Jessica saw Sparky a block ahead of her, running back and forth in a frenzy. He was too scared to bark, but he was yelping now and then, his little voice sounding pitiful.

Mr. Glennon probably hadn't let him out on purpose, Jessica realized. Sparky must have been frightened by the thunder and bolted when Mr. Glennon wasn't looking.

"I've got to catch him," Jessica told herself as she raced after him. No matter how scared she felt to be out in the storm, Sparky was obviously more scared. She had to save the little dog before he ran off for good! She chased Sparky down the block, getting farther and farther from home.

"Jessica! Jessica!"

What in the world? Jessica stopped running and turned around, rain lashing her face. "Who is it?" she called into the dark night.

A figure in a yellow raincoat skidded to a stop in front of her. It was a girl—Jessica could tell that much. The girl pushed her hood back, revealing a familiar face. "It's *me*, Jessica. Where are you going?"

"Elizabeth! What are you doing here?" Jessica yelled, straining to be heard above another earsplitting crash of thunder.

"I was looking out the window and I saw you sneak out. I know you're grounded, so I want to bring you back before Mom and Dad find out and you get into trouble!" Elizabeth explained. "So forget about going to Lila's for a party, or shopping at the mall, or whatever you were going to do. It's eight o'clock and we're supposed to be home for the night, doing our homework—"

"I'm not going back home—not yet!" Jessica replied. "I can't!"

"But you're grounded," Elizabeth said. "Come on, Jessica—nothing's worth this." She stepped forward and took hold of her twin's arm.

Jessica shook off Elizabeth's grip. "I told you, I can't go! I saw Mr. Glennon's dog out here. He's lost and scared and he doesn't know where he is! I have to find him!"

"Later," Elizabeth said, "after the storm! Come on, Jessica—I'm working so hard to get you *un*-grounded. Don't blow it for me now!"

Jessica stared at her, dumbfounded. "What are you talking about? How are you getting me ungrounded?" She shook her head. "Don't answer that. I don't want to hear any more of your lies!"

"But Jessica, I was only lying because you needed me to," Elizabeth protested. She raked a hand through her wet hair. "I was helping you get rid of all the problems I created. And it's working, isn't it? Aaron forgave you, Lila forgave you, Janet forgave you—"

"Well, guess what, Elizabeth. I *don't* forgive *you*," Jessica said angrily. "You've meddled in my life for the last time."

"The last time?" Elizabeth's forehead creased with concern. "What do you mean?"

"One minute you're telling the truth, the next you're lying through your teeth," Jessica accused her twin. "I can't trust you, Elizabeth!"

"I don't know what you're talking about," Elizabeth said. "I'm only trying to help!"

"Making all these convoluted plans—that's helping me?" Jessica demanded.

"I didn't plan anything! I just said what came into my head!" Elizabeth yelled to be heard over the loud thunder.

"Well, quit talking, then!" Jessica said as a bolt of lightning flashed across the sky. "And stop trying to help me! Leave me alone!"

Elizabeth took a step backward. She just stood there for a minute. Finally she said, "OK. I-I'm sorry, Jessica." Her eyes were watery, but Jessica couldn't tell whether she was about to cry or it was only the rain.

Before Jessica could say anything else, Elizabeth turned and ran back toward their house. Her feet splashed in giant puddles as she sprinted down the sidewalk.

Jessica groaned. She hadn't meant for that to sound so harsh. All she meant was that she couldn't go back inside her house, not now—not when Sparky was out in the cold, wet night. He needed her.

But the look on Elizabeth's face when she'd told her to get lost . . . it was so sad, it nearly broke Jessica's heart. *Why did I have to say that? Why did it come out sounding so mean? Anyway, I'm the one who made her either brutally honest or brutally dishonest. I'm the one who wishes I'd never wished anything!*

Jessica stared up at the dull, cloudy night sky as a crack of thunder rattled the ground, starting car alarms up and down the block. Before she followed Sparky, she had one last wish to make. There were no falling stars, though. *Maybe I can wish on lightning,* Jessica thought. *It's worth a shot.*

She watched the sky carefully, waiting for the right moment. Finally a jagged flash of lightning illuminated the trees and houses around her. "I just wish things would get back to normal!" Jessica cried at the top of her lungs.

"Sparky!" Jessica called. "Sparky, wait up!"

She had come around the corner just in time to see Sparky's little white tail disappear into a garage. Jessica glanced at the mailbox and address as she ran up the house's driveway.

Jacobson was the name written in block letters on the mailbox.

This is Denny's house! Jessica realized with a pang of panic. She'd have to be careful not to let him overhear her. He was probably still angry about her deceptive matchmaking efforts.

"Sparky?" Jessica whispered. "Sparky, are you in here?" She stepped through the door into the garage. Searching around for a light switch, her hand knocked into a tall can of spray paint. It crashed to the ground, clattered against the cement floor, and rolled into the corner.

Jessica winced at the loud noise. "OK, Sparky. Sorry about that. Didn't mean to scare you," she whispered. "Will you come out now? I can't see you in the dark."

A tiny whine that sounded as though it came from a puppy was the only reply. From the sound of it, the dog was hiding underneath the car.

"Sparky? Is that you?" Jessica asked, purposely keeping her voice low and soothing. She began creeping around the edge of the Jeep. "You know, if I were you, I'd hide too. That storm was a loud one. But it's moving out of town now." Jessica moved to the front of the car. "You could come out and be safe with me. I'll take you straight home to Mr. Glennon, and you can curl up on your little dog bed and—"

As she tried to maneuver her way around the car's hood, Jessica's hip bumped into a tower of cardboard boxes at the front of the garage. The boxes toppled to the ground.

"Aagh!" Jessica cried as the boxes fell onto her, burying her in cardboard. "Sparky, run!" she cried as the boxes continued to fall, one of them landing right on her head. Luckily, they were all empty.

All of a sudden a bright overhead light switched on.

"Jessica? What are *you* doing here?"

Thirteen

◇

Jessica stepped out from behind the Jeep. "Um, hi, Denny. What's up?"

"You're in my garage, in the middle of a huge thunderstorm, and you're asking *me* what's up?" Denny walked over toward her. "What in the world are you doing in here? Stealing my brother's car or something?"

"Ha, ha, ha," Jessica laughed nervously. "That's a good one. Stealing your brother's car. See, I don't even know how to drive, and—"

"Yeah. I *know*," Denny said, sounding irritated. "That was a *joke*. So why are you here?"

"Would you believe I was chasing a dog?" Jessica said, giving Denny a bright smile.

"You were?" Denny asked. "You mean that dog you were walking the other day?"

"Exactly!" Jessica said, and bit her lip nervously. "Sparky. That cute little Jack Russell terrier. I guess he's afraid of storms," she explained. "I saw him run by our house, and I've been chasing him ever since."

"From your house to here?" Denny stared at her with admiration—or was it amazement? Jessica wondered. "That's a long way! Maybe two miles."

"Otherwise known as three point two kilometers," Jessica joked. "Every time I started to catch up to Sparky, there was another lightning bolt or a crash of thunder, and he'd take off all over again. Until we got to your block. I don't know why, but he ran straight for your garage. He must think it's safe here or something."

She crouched down, peering under the Jeep. Directly under the center of the car was a small, wet dog. "There he is!" Jessica said quietly, pointing.

Denny bent down on his knees, looking underneath the car. "It *is* Sparky. Wow. He's soaked."

"I know," Jessica said. "Hey, Sparky. Come here! We'll dry you off," she offered.

Sparky whimpered.

"He's really freaked out," Denny observed. "I'd go under there and get him, but I think it would only end up scaring him more."

"Well, I can't just leave him here," Jessica said. "I

feel responsible for him. We should call Mr. Glennon and let him know Sparky's OK. Then maybe he can come over to get him."

"Good idea," Denny agreed. "Come on in the house!"

Jessica hung up the telephone with a loud sigh. "No answer. Mr. Glennon's not home. He must be out looking for Sparky."

"Hmmm." Denny drummed his fingers against the kitchen counter. "There has to be some way we can calm Sparky down without waiting for Mr. Glennon."

"I don't know," Jessica said. "That little dog is so unhappy right now! He's been yelping and whimpering for half an hour. And he must be freezing cold."

"Well, he's inside now—safe and sound," Denny said. "And the storm is nearly over. If we could just get him to come out on his own, without forcing him, he'd probably calm down a whole lot."

"We need something to coax him out," Jessica said, trying not to stare at the collection of magnets on the Jacobsons' refrigerator. One of them was holding up a picture of Denny and Janet from a Christmas party the previous winter. All of the stuff about getting them back together seemed far away now. In fact, everything about the picnic seemed unreal. Jessica couldn't care less about whom she went with or whether Janet and Denny ever spoke to each other again. All she wanted to do was help Sparky.

"I wish we had a dog biscuit or a treat," Denny mused. "Only we don't have a dog. So we don't have any of that stuff around."

"Wait!" Jessica jumped off the stool. "He likes that junk OK, but remember what he really loved? Crumb cake! He was crazy for your crumb cake that day when you were coming out of Some Crumb! He ate it right out of your hand, remember?"

Denny snapped his fingers. "That's right! He went wild for that. Come on, Jessica. The rain's let up a little bit. I'll ride my brother's bike, and you can ride mine. We need to make an emergency trip!"

Jessica climbed off Denny's bike and leaned it against the window of Some Crumb Bakery. The streets and sidewalks were shiny with water, but the moon had begun to peek through the clouds. It was dark, but not half as scary as it had been an hour before.

Jessica followed Denny into the bakery, shaking rainwater off her coat as she walked through the door. A bell jingled as they entered the bakery.

"Kids! What are you doing out on a night like this?" Martha, the bakery's owner, called to them from behind the counter. "I was about to close, but there was a last-minute rush."

"A rush?" Jessica asked, looking around the bakery at the empty tables. There was one person at the counter ahead of them, busily stuffing a box of cookies and a cake box into her plastic tote bag.

"With weather like this, I consider three customers a crowd," Martha said warmly. "Now what can I get you?"

The girl in front of them turned around, and Jessica gasped. It was Janet!

"Excuse me," she said. "But in my book, three is a crowd anytime. Especially when the other two people are you!"

"J-Janet," Denny sputtered.

"Hi, Janet," Jessica said. "Look, this isn't as weird as it seems. See, Mr. Glennon's dog—"

Janet glared at her. "You used that story before, Jessica. Try to work on some new material while you guys are enjoying your snack." Her lip trembling, Janet shoved past them, heading for the door.

Does she think we're on a date or something? Jessica wondered. She watched as Janet paused at the door to put her raincoat back on. Janet brushed at her eyes, as if she were wiping something off her face.

Tears? Jessica mused. Could Janet Howell be *crying?* She seemed to be searching for something in her tote bag.

Probably a tissue, Jessica thought. *I should go over and offer her one.* As nasty as Janet had been the past few days, she didn't deserve to have her heart broken by thinking something that wasn't true. Denny was a cool guy and everything, but Jessica would never go after a friend's boyfriend.

"So, then, have you decided what you'd like?" Martha stood by the case containing the few remaining baked goods from that day. "Rainy-night special—everything's fifty percent off." She wiped her hands on her apron.

"Well, uh . . ." Denny sounded as uncomfortable as Jessica felt. "We came in because we need something for a dog."

"A dog?" Martha peered into the glass case. "I'm sold out of my special bagel biscuits, but—"

"No," Jessica interrupted. "What we actually need is a crumb cake. This dog—he's scared and hiding, and we want him to come out. So we thought we'd hold out some crumb cake and—"

"I hate to disappoint you," Martha said, "but I don't have any crumb cakes left. Gee, what a shame. This really sounds like an emergency. But I just sold the last one to my other customer over there." She pointed to the door.

"We're desperate," Jessica said. "Is there any

way you could ask for it back?" she whispered to Martha. *Because if I ask Janet for her cake, she'll probably smash it over my head.*

"Sorry, kids—you're on your own," Martha said with a shrug.

"I'll ask her," Denny declared. He marched over to Janet, looking determined. "Look, Janet, I know you hate me right now. But could you forget about that for a second? I need your help."

She just glared at him, her eyes red. She didn't say a word.

"I have to have that cake. It's not for me, OK? It's for this frightened dog we found," Denny explained. "I'm sure you want the cake too, but would you please sell it to me? I'll pay you double." He took out his wallet and pulled out a ten-dollar bill. "You never have to talk to me again, I promise. And I'm really sorry about everything. That day we were supposed to meet here . . . I blew it, OK? Just please do me this one favor."

Janet stared at the box in her hand. Her mouth was turned downward in a frown that seemed to soften after Denny's speech. She glanced at him, and Jessica could see that her eyes were full of tears.

This time they really are going to make up! Jessica thought excitedly. *Without any help from me!*

Janet suddenly shoved the small, square box at him. "Here, you can have it." Then she turned and ran out of the bakery toward a waiting car.

Jessica hurried over to Denny. He was staring at the top of the white box with a stunned expression. Jessica followed his gaze.

On top of the box Janet had written, *To Denny. I'm sorry I didn't listen. Janet.*

Denny shoved the cake box into Jessica's arms. Then he ran out the door, calling, "Janet! Wait!"

Jessica turned to look at the bakery shop owner and shrugged. "True love. What can you do?"

"Thanks for waiting for me." Denny climbed onto his brother's bicycle after strapping the cake box to his metal rack. "I hope I didn't take too long—I really don't like the thought of Sparky hiding under that car."

"It's OK," Jessica said, pedaling down the sidewalk beside him. Denny's bike light shone on the path in front of them. It was nearly nine o'clock. Jessica needed to get home! "So, um . . . how did it go?" she asked timidly.

"It went great," Denny said. "She said that she was only buying the crumb cake for me in the first place, to apologize, since she knows it's my favorite. Then when we came in, she thought we were . . . well . . . on a date, kind of."

"You and me? On a date?" Jessica laughed. "No way."

"Pretty crazy, huh?" Denny shook his head.

"But I guess since I asked her to meet me here once, she thought it was where I took all my dates or something. Like I have any other dates. Anyway, once I explained about Sparky and apologized for what made us fight in the first place—well, the bottom line is, we're *not* fighting anymore. And we *are* going to the picnic together."

"That's awesome!" Jessica said, straining to keep up with Denny, who was at least a foot taller than she was. "Wow. I'm so glad we ran into her. I was kind of worried when she threw that cake at you."

"She didn't *throw* it," Denny said with a laugh.

"No, maybe not. But that's what I *thought* she was going to do," Jessica pointed out. *Actually, I thought she was going to throw it at me. But now that she and Denny are together, happily ever after, or at least until next week, maybe she'll quit being such a grouch and forget all about me.*

"Well," Jessica said with a sigh, "I'm glad she's forgiven *you* anyway."

"I'm sure she'll get over it," Denny said, coasting to a stop in his driveway. "You were only trying to help, right?"

"Right," Jessica said, a shiver running through her. That was exactly what Elizabeth had said to her earlier that night. She'd told her twin that she never wanted her help again.

Maybe she'd reacted too strongly. After all, Elizabeth's intentions had probably been as good as hers. No, she realized, they'd probably been much better.

But she'd have to deal with that later.

Jessica leaned Denny's bike against the garage and ran into the garage after him. "Sparky!" she called. "Sparky, we're back," she cooed. "Will you come out now? The storm's all gone."

"And we brought you something." Denny gave the string circling the cake box a snap. Then he pulled open the top and lifted out the round crumb cake. "Last time I only had a mini crumb cake, Sparky. But this is the *real* deal."

Jessica got down on her hands and knees and peered under the Jeep. Sparky was still sitting right in the middle. He was shaking—whether from cold or fear, Jessica wasn't sure.

Denny broke off a small piece of the cake and took a bite. "Mmm, good. Crumb cake is one of my favorites too, Sparky." He sat on the floor. "I figure if we act relaxed, he'll feel more relaxed," he told Jessica.

She nodded. "Wasn't that storm the worst?" Jessica crawled over to Denny and broke off a piece of cake for Sparky. "But it's over now. Good thing too. I have to be getting home!" She reached under the car, the piece of cake propped in her hand. "Sparky? Want some?"

There was a loud bark, and when Jessica peered under the car again, she saw Sparky's soggy tail swishing back and forth on the cement floor. It was still so wet that he was leaving a trail.

"Good boy, Sparky. You hungry?" Jessica pushed the hunk of crumb cake farther toward him.

Jessica heard toenails clicking on the floor. A second later the piece of cake disappeared from sight. Then Sparky poked his head out from under the Jeep. He was licking his chops.

"All right, Sparky! Way to go!" Denny broke off another small piece of cake for the dog.

Sparky ate it in one bite, then walked closer to Jessica, as if he wanted to be petted. She reached out to rub his head. Sparky shook his body back and forth, drying off—spraying water all over Jessica!

"Good thing you kept your raincoat on," Denny said with a laugh.

Jessica started laughing too. Normally she would have been horrified, but she was already so drenched, she didn't care. Anyway, Sparky was safe—that was all that mattered.

"Come on," Denny said, getting to his feet. "I'll get my mom to give you *and* Sparky a ride home."

"I hope her car has waterproof seats," Jessica told him, giggling.

"I'll get some towels. You get the rest of the

cake," Denny said, picking up the box from the garage floor.

"No, you keep it," Jessica told him as Sparky stopped shaking and stood on his hind legs, begging for more cake. She scratched behind his ears instead. "You might want to hold on to the box. Right?"

Denny looked down at Janet's handwriting on the lid. "Yeah. You're right. Thanks, Jessica."

"No problem." She smiled at Denny. "Hey, you know what? Mr. Glennon is going to be so happy to see Sparky, I don't think I'll have to earn any more extra credit for the rest of the year!"

"I don't think you'll have to go to *class*," Denny said with a laugh.

Jessica, I couldn't be more grateful. Thank you so, so much. You practically saved Sparky's life, and I'll never forget this.

Mr. Glennon's words echoed in Jessica's head as she walked up the sidewalk to her house. Her parents were going to be absolutely furious with her for running out of the house the way she had. But one person was happy she'd taken the risk. At least Mr. Glennon was on her side.

She opened the door slowly, glancing at the clock on the kitchen wall. Jessica cringed. It was nearly nine-thirty. She never stayed out that late on a school night, and especially not in the middle of a storm.

"Jessica!" Mrs. Wakefield rushed toward the door, her face creased with concern. "Where were you? We were so worried!"

Jessica closed the door behind her. "Didn't Elizabeth explain where I was?"

"No, she didn't," Mr. Wakefield said, rising from the sofa. "She's upstairs working on her homework. Which is where you should be! You're grounded—again! What's more, running around in a storm is dangerous, Jessica!"

"I know," Jessica said. "And I'm really sorry, but I had to do it. I saw Mr. Glennon's little dog out there, and he was scared and lost. So I tried to catch him, only he ended up at the Jacobsons'. Denny and I went to get a crumb cake at Some Crumb, and we ran into Janet—"

"You went out for a crumb cake? With friends? In the middle of a thunderstorm?" Mrs. Wakefield asked.

"I don't want to hear any of your stories, Jessica." Mr. Wakefield stared at her with a stern expression.

"It's not a story—it's the truth!" Jessica said. "Please, you have to believe me."

"And you have to get upstairs and change out of those wet clothes before you catch cold." Mrs. Wakefield pointed to the stairs. "We can talk more about this tomorrow. Right now I want you to get to bed. I'm worried about you, Jessica."

"So am I," Mr. Wakefield said. "I'm worried that you don't understand how serious this is. Jessica, you could have been hurt tonight, or—"

"But I wasn't," Jessica argued. "And I only did it for Sparky."

"I'm sorry, Jessica," her mother said. "But we've heard enough. Good night."

Jessica slowly trudged up to her room and closed the door. Her parents didn't believe a word she said anymore. Not even when she was telling the truth!

Jessica glanced out her bedroom window. The sky had cleared, and a thousand tiny stars twinkled in the distance. Almost as a reflex, Jessica began to search the sky for another falling star.

Nope, Jessica thought, turning away from the window. *Not tonight. I'm through making wishes.*

She quickly changed into her pajamas and crawled into bed, pulling the covers snugly around her neck. She'd never felt so exhausted in her life!

Fourteen

◇

"Jessica! Jessica, wake up! You're going to be late for school!"

At the sound of her mother's voice, Jessica slowly opened her eyes. It was Friday morning. She winced at the bright sunlight streaming through the window across her bed. It was hard to believe there had been such a violent thunderstorm the night before. The sky was a clear blue, and there wasn't a cloud to be seen.

Jessica sat up, shoving the covers aside. If she didn't hurry, she'd be late for school. She was never late on Fridays—it was her favorite day of the week. Not counting Saturday and Sunday, of course. She pulled her terry cloth robe off the hook on the back of the door and headed into the bathroom she shared with Elizabeth.

Halfway there she remembered what had happened the day before. Sergio had made her hair as awful as Lila's! She was a curly mess.

Jessica raced to her closet and reached up to the top shelf, where she kept her cold-weather clothes. She pulled out everything, tossing wool scarves and hats onto her bed. She'd have to find an outfit she could wear a hat with—for the next several months. She stared at the four hats on her bed. She was going to need a lot more of them if she wanted to leave the house more often than four times a week.

With a sigh she headed for the bathroom again. She switched on the light, then turned on the shower. She was about to step in when she decided she'd better look at her hair. She had to assess the damage.

She turned toward the mirror, afraid to look.

Wait a second, she thought, staring at her reflection. *What happened to my hair?*

It was straight! Boringly, traditionally, wonderfully straight!

Jessica suddenly remembered Sergio calling after her as she ran out of the salon: "Whatever you do, do not wash the hair for three days or the curl will not hold!"

She hadn't washed it. But she had run around in the pouring rain all night.

"Yes!" Jessica shouted. "No more Octopus Head!"

*   *   *

"How's the omelette?" Jessica stood over the breakfast table, peering down at her sister's plate.

"Pretty good," Elizabeth replied, glancing up at her. Then she went back to reading the morning newspaper. She didn't feel like talking to Jessica. If her twin thought she could blame Elizabeth for everything that went wrong in her life, she could forget it.

"Pretty good? That's it?" Jessica stared at her. "The eggs aren't too cold?" she asked. "Mom didn't add too much cheese, or not enough spinach?"

Elizabeth shook her head, taking another bite. *Go away!* she thought. *Leave me alone!*

"They're not the most magnificently fluffy eggs you've ever eaten?" Jessica pressed. "You don't think they're so delicious that Mom should start her own cooking school or—"

Elizabeth shook her head. "No! It's just a really good omelette. Anyway, I don't know why I'm even talking to you after the way you yelled at me last night." She pushed back her chair and stood up.

"I'm sorry," Jessica said. "I didn't mean that I didn't want your help *ever*. I was just upset because—"

"Yeah, whatever." Elizabeth wasn't about to believe anything Jessica told her. "You know what, Jessica? Until you start being up front with me, I don't even want to hear it."

"Hmmm. You *sound* normal," Jessica said, peering into Elizabeth's eyes. "You *look* normal."

"I am normal! *You're* the one who's acting weird," Elizabeth said, stalking over to the dishwasher with her dirty plate.

Jessica followed her. "So does that mean your head is clear this morning? Or do you feel like you're in a trance? Or—"

"It means that you're bugging me and I'm going to be late for school!" Elizabeth cried. *Really*, she wondered. *What's gotten into Jessica lately?*

Jessica walked down the hallway toward her locker later that morning, whistling happily to herself. She couldn't help it. She felt as if her life was back on track. Elizabeth was mad at her, as usual. And having her hairstyle back proved it. Things were great!

She opened her locker and started sorting through her books. As she stood there she heard Bruce and Lila talking. They were standing at Lila's locker, a few yards away.

"So, Lila," Bruce was saying, "you know how I said I had a date for the picnic? Actually, it didn't end up working out for me."

"Gee, that's too bad," Lila said without a trace of sympathy in her voice.

"Yeah. Well, see, first I had two dates. But that was too many, and I realized that wasn't really fair to anyone. I mean, I should give my undivided attention to my date or she won't be happy. So I dumped one of the girls," Bruce explained.

Jessica rolled her eyes. She could just see Bruce bragging about dumping her for the rest of the school year.

"And then, surprise, surprise, your other date dumped *you*," Lila said.

"Well, er, not exactly," Bruce mumbled.

"Yes, exactly," Lila said. "I already heard about it from Christy herself."

Jessica put her hand over her mouth, stifling a laugh. *Go, Lila!* she thought.

"Anyway, that's not the point. The point is that your hair looks really nice today," Bruce went on. "I'm glad you got rid of that perm thing."

"Thanks for the compliment," Lila said dryly.

"Yeah. So now that you look good again, and I'm free, I was thinking this works out sort of perfectly. So how about going to the picnic with me next week?" Bruce asked.

"You know what, Bruce? That's incredibly flattering," Lila said in a sickeningly sweet voice. "But I really don't appreciate being your *third* choice. And I already have a date, someone who asked me a long time ago."

"Oh, yeah?" Bruce grumbled. "Who?"

"Not that it's any of your business, but Mike McCluskey asked me days ago, while you were busy lining up your two other dates," Lila informed him. "Sorry, Bruce! Looks like you'll have to go solo."

Jessica snickered.

"What's so funny?"

Jessica whirled around. Aaron was standing behind her.

"It's Lila. She just told off Bruce." Jessica looked up nervously at Aaron. She knew that Aaron thought everything was OK between them, but Jessica still felt weird about the way she had treated him.

"I'm sure he deserved it," Aaron said.

"He did. But then, I kind of did too," Jessica admitted. "Listen, Aaron. I'm really sorry about the other day and how I agreed to go to the picnic with Bruce instead of you."

"Huh?" Aaron looked confused. "But Elizabeth said—"

"Elizabeth was lying," Jessica told him. She heaved a deep sigh. Why was coming clean so painful?

"Why would she do that?" Aaron's brow was furrowed. "That's not like her. You didn't *ask* her to lie for you, did you?"

"No!" Jessica said. "Well, not on purpose. Anyway, that doesn't matter. The fact is that she did lie. I did say I'd go to the picnic with Bruce. But not because I like him! It was for a really dumb reason."

Aaron folded his arms across his chest. "Such as?"

"Lila and I had this competition going, for who could get a date to the picnic first. I was afraid she was going to win!" Jessica said. "And the consequences of losing . . . well, they were pretty harsh. I know I shouldn't have done what I did. But I had to get a date before Lila. It was a matter of—"

"Life and death?" Aaron interrupted. "Come on, Jessica. You don't really expect me to believe that."

"No. But it was a matter of Janet Howell. That's really all I can say," Jessica told him. "I'm sorry. It was all incredibly dumb."

Aaron didn't say anything. He stared at the floor, kicking a small pebble around like a soccer ball. "I can't believe you'd even think of going with Bruce. For any reason. You knew I was going to ask you."

"No, I didn't," Jessica said. "I mean, I *hoped*, but . . . what can I say? I had a deadline."

"Well . . . I'm still kind of upset. But I guess if you don't really *like* Bruce—"

"I don't!" Jessica said. "Believe me."

"Then it's OK." Aaron shrugged. "I forgive you."

"You do? Well, thanks," Jessica said. That was another reason she liked Aaron so much. He was so understanding about her faults!

"You know what? I just ran into Denny. He said that he and Janet got back together last night," Aaron said. "Something about seeing her at a bakery in the middle of that big thunderstorm. I didn't really get the whole story, but she apologized, so they're back on for the picnic."

"Oh?" Jessica said. "Really?" Jessica didn't want to admit she'd had anything to do with that. Being too involved in Denny and Janet's love life was what had gotten her in trouble in the first place. Well, one of the things anyway.

"Yeah. And—look, I really admire you for sticking by Janet and being such a good friend to her when she was down," Aaron said. "But since she and Denny are going to the picnic together, do you think maybe you could go with me now?"

Jessica felt a flutter of excitement. "I'd love to go to the picnic with you! Thanks for asking—again." She smiled at Aaron. Everything was going to work out after all—just the way she had wanted it to from the start. She'd sit with Aaron at the picnic, and dance with Aaron at the picnic, and—

Oh, no, Jessica suddenly realized, *I won't.* She slumped against her locker with a loud sigh.

"What's the matter?" Aaron asked, looking concerned. He reached out to catch Jessica's arm. "You look like you're about to faint."

"I'm OK. But . . . I can't go to the picnic with you," Jessica said.

"Why not?" Aaron looked crushed.

"I want to!" Jessica explained. "It's just that my parents grounded me. No social events for a whole month!"

"Oh." Aaron scuffed the floor with the toe of his suede sneaker. "Do you think there's any chance they'll change their minds?"

Jessica remembered how angry her parents had been about her "technical" B and sneaking out in the storm. "I kind of doubt it."

"How can they make you miss the end-of-the-year picnic? Everyone goes," Aaron argued.

"Maybe you could call them for me and point that out," Jessica suggested with a half smile.

"Hi, guys." Janet slid into a seat at the Unicorner. "Did you see my new bracelet?" She held her wrist out in front of everyone, shoving their glasses and trays aside to make room for her arm.

"We saw it," Lila sighed.

"About five times already," Jessica added under her breath.

"I still can't believe Denny kept this the whole time we were fighting," Janet said. "He was going to give it to me that day at Some Crumb. He said he never even *thought* about returning it, even though we weren't speaking to each other for days."

Jessica wasn't going to say anything, but she found that a bit hard to believe. She was pretty sure that Denny had *thought* more than once about returning the bracelet. It was probably nonreturnable, she thought with a wicked smile.

Janet turned her wrist back and forth, admiring the silver bracelet. "Isn't he the greatest?"

"Whatever happened to Denny being a liar?" Mary asked.

"Well. Some people do lie, of course," Janet said. She glanced around the cafeteria. "Take Bruce Patman, for starters. But Denny's nothing like him."

Jessica couldn't help smiling. "You know what, Janet? You're right about that. Denny is a really nice guy. Much nicer than Bruce."

She felt something slam into her calf, and she grabbed her leg. "Ow!"

"Don't encourage her," Lila whispered fiercely.

"Thanks a lot, Jessica! Now we won't hear about anything else all day!" Mandy said under her breath.

"Like you were going to anyway," Jessica replied. "Anyway, can I help it if I found out Denny's really cool?"

Another shoe banged into her leg.

"Ow!" Jessica cried. "Quit it!" she said to Lila.

"That was me." Janet gave her a superior smile. "Don't get any ideas," she warned. "Denny Jacobson's all mine."

"And you're all his, believe me," Jessica said. *Thank goodness! Because I've had about all I can take of you!* Was this the thanks she got for patching up Janet's love life? Two giant bruises on her shins?

"We're all going to have such an awesome time at the picnic next week," Mandy said. "I can't wait."

"Me either," Lila said, gazing across the room at Mike.

"Jessica? How come you haven't said anything about your date for the picnic? Didn't you get one?" Janet snickered.

Jessica gripped her fork tightly. "Of course I got one," she said. *I just can't go, that's all,* she thought, her heart sinking. *And when Janet finds that out, I'll never hear the end of it. . . .*

Fifteen

◇

"Jessica? Are you home?"

Jessica opened her bedroom door a crack. Her mother was calling to her from the kitchen. "I have to go, Lila. I'll call you later, OK?" she said into the telephone.

"Just remember. *Beg*," Lila instructed.

Jessica pressed the Off button on the cordless telephone and set it on her bed. "I'm here, Mom!" she yelled, running downstairs.

When she got to the bottom of the stairs, both her mother and father were waiting for her.

"You guys got home early," she said. Usually both her parents worked until five o'clock. It was only quarter to five. "Is everything all right?"

"Yes. We left work early because we had a

personal conference with one of your teachers after school," Mr. Wakefield told her.

"You did?" Jessica asked. "But it isn't parent-teacher day."

"I know it isn't. But sometimes things come up that can't wait," her mother said. "And that was the case with this teacher."

Jessica was almost afraid to ask the next question. "Which one was it?"

"Mr. Glennon." Mrs. Wakefield put her purse on the kitchen table and slid onto a chair. "Have a seat, Jessica."

Jessica gulped. She could forget about begging now. She might as well go upstairs to her room for the remainder of the school year. "Um . . . I can explain," she said, stalling for time.

"That's OK. Mr. Glennon already explained everything," Mr. Wakefield said, grabbing a carton of orange juice from the refrigerator. "Anyone else want some?"

Jessica shook her head. Who could have a snack at a time like this?

Mr. Wakefield poured a glass of juice and sat down beside Jessica. "Mr. Glennon told us what you did," he said, looking right at Jessica.

"He . . . he did?" Jessica managed.

"Yes. And we're very proud of you," Mrs. Wakefield said. "Going out into a thunderstorm to rescue his little dog and bringing him over to his house—that was a very nice thing to do. Not to mention brave. I'm sorry we didn't believe you last night. I didn't know about Sparky's fondness for crumb cake. We should have taken you at your word."

"Oh. Well, thanks," Jessica said. She frowned, feeling confused. "Is that why he called a parent-teacher conference?"

"Oh, no. That was just a bonus," Mr. Wakefield said. "The real news was even more important."

"It . . . it was?" Jessica said, her voice cracking.

"Yes. Mr. Glennon went over the math tests again. He discovered that he'd made an error when he was grading them," her mother said. "His correction key was wrong. So instead of the C he originally gave you—"

"You actually got a B!" Mr. Wakefield said happily. "Without any extra credit at all!"

"I did?" Jessica sat up, stunned.

Her father was smiling at her. "Not only that, but Mr. Glennon said you've been trying really hard recently. You're making excellent progress, according to him. He wanted to let us know you've already got a solid B in the class—and you're not that far from an A. You might get an A at the end of the year if you keep up the good work."

"Wow," Jessica said, looking at her mother. "I had no idea."

Mrs. Wakefield laughed. "I'm sure you had *some* idea. And as of right now, you can consider yourself ungrounded," her mother told her.

Jessica's eyes widened. "You're kidding! No, you're not kidding. Tell me you're not kidding!"

Mr. Wakefield looked at his wife. "Why is not being grounded more exciting than getting an A in math?"

"Because of the picnic! Now I can go with Aaron!" Jessica picked up the telephone and rapidly dialed Aaron's number.

"Really, Ned. Don't you remember anything about being twelve?" Jessica's mother shook her head, laughing.

"Hi, Aaron? This is Jessica. Guess what? I can go to the picnic after all!"

Jessica bounced up the stairs. She had only one more thing to do. But it was probably the most important thing of all.

"Elizabeth? Can I come in?" Jessica knocked on her twin's bedroom door. She could see the glow of the computer screen from where she stood in the hallway. She could hear Elizabeth's fingers tapping on the keyboard as she typed.

"Sure, come on in," Elizabeth replied over her shoulder.

"I hate to interrupt," Jessica said, stepping into her sister's room. "But I had to apologize."

"It's OK. Have a seat." Elizabeth spun around in her desk chair, facing her twin.

Jessica perched on the edge of the bed. "I'm sorry about what happened last night. I didn't mean to yell at you. I know you were only trying to help me." She shook her head. "And I could have used your help. I was just so wrapped up in my own problems that I didn't know what to do."

"It's all right," Elizabeth said. "I forgive you."

Jessica's eyebrows flew up. "Just like that?" Jessica snapped her fingers. "Shouldn't I apologize for a couple more hours?"

Elizabeth laughed. "No, thanks!"

"Really? Because I was awfully mean," Jessica said. "I don't think I should get off that easily."

Elizabeth waved her hand in the air. "I've already forgotten about it. I'm too busy working on this essay for Mr. Bowman."

"What's it about?" Jessica asked, peering at the computer screen.

"It's supposed to be on the power of words," Elizabeth said. "Mr. Bowman asked me to write it two weeks ago, for a nationwide contest. But I was having the hardest time coming up with any ideas."

"You?" Jessica asked with a wry smile.

"Hey, it happens to the best of us." Elizabeth tossed a floppy disk at her. "Anyway, I finally

thought of something. The idea hit me last night—
like a bolt of lightning."

"R-Really?" Jessica asked. *Speaking of lightning . . .
no, I don't even want to think about it. It's too weird!*

"Yeah. The idea was right in front of me. I decided to write about my experiences over the past
few days," Elizabeth said. "I'm calling it 'Truth or
Consequences.' What do you think?"

The back of Jessica's neck prickled. Truth . . .
lies . . . consequences. What was Elizabeth writing—her life story? Jessica had already decided
that she wasn't going to make any more wishes.
Not without thinking them through a lot more
carefully first!

"Sounds good," Jessica said, standing up and
slowly backing out of the room.

"Wait—where are you going?" Elizabeth asked.
"I wanted to tell you more about my paper."

"Oh, you know me, Elizabeth. I can't really get
into writing," Jessica said. *Especially not about truth
and consequences! I've had more than enough of that
lately!*

"Amy, catch!" Elizabeth tossed a Frisbee toward
her friend.

Sweet Valley Park was full of students—some
playing touch football and Frisbee, some lounging
on blankets. A band was warming up on the stage
near the picnic tables, where parents and teachers

were setting out plates of food and barbecuing hamburgers and chicken. The sun was shining brightly—it was a beautiful day for the end-of-the-year picnic.

Amy leaped for the flying blue disc, jumping just inches above Ken to catch it. "Got it!" she yelled.

"Only because I let you have that one," Ken told her. "Hey, Todd—go long!" He snatched the Frisbee from Amy's grasp and flung it over Todd's head.

"Well, *he* won't be back for a while," Elizabeth commented to Winston and Grace as Todd sprinted after the Frisbee. The wind had caught it and was carrying the disc yards beyond him.

"He might set a land speed record, though," Winston joked.

"Elizabeth, I just read your essay! It's wonderful." Mr. Bowman walked toward Elizabeth with a big smile on his face. He was wearing striped Bermuda shorts, a T-shirt, and beat-up sneakers. He looked very relaxed.

"Really? You think so?" Elizabeth asked.

"No, it's terrible." Winston rolled his eyes. "Come on! It's written by *Elizabeth Wakefield*."

"Yeah, but . . . this one I wasn't so sure about," Elizabeth confessed, her face turning pink.

"Neither was I." Mr. Bowman shook his head. "First you told me you didn't get it done and didn't want to write it. Then you said you did write it but your dog ate it—"

Grace put her hand over her mouth, stifling a giggle.

"Anyway, I wasn't sure what was going on," Mr. Bowman finished.

"To tell you the truth, Mr. Bowman, neither was I," Elizabeth said. "This has been a really weird week."

"Well, all's well that ends well, I suppose," Mr. Bowman said. "And this is one terrific essay. How did you ever learn so much about truth and consequences?"

"Oh, you know," Elizabeth said with a smile. "Living with Jessica."

Jessica sat on a plaid blanket, her legs crossed underneath her. She was wearing jean shorts and a white T-shirt. "*This* is the life."

"I'll say." Lila leaned back against a tree trunk and let out a contented sigh.

"Too bad all the boys are playing football," Janet said with a frown.

"I don't care," Jessica said. "They'll be back as soon as the band starts playing, right?"

"And I'm having a perfectly fine time just hanging out with you guys," Ellen said with a smile.

"Exactly," Mandy agreed. "In fact, I—wait a minute. Oh, no." She held her arm out straight, pointing ahead of her. "Look at Mr. Clark!"

Jessica turned around and saw their principal heading toward them. Instead of his usual business suit, he was wearing jeans and a T-shirt. He even had sunglasses on! But that wasn't the most shocking part of it.

"He's *not*," Mandy said breathlessly.

"He *is*," Janet said.

As Mr. Clark came closer Jessica stared at the T-shirt. It was hot pink, with big orange letters on the front. The color combination was horrid. But what the T-shirt said was even more appalling.

"Hello, girls. Are you having fun?" Mr. Clark stopped in front of their collection of picnic blankets and gazed down at them.

"Mr. *Clark*? Where did you *get* that?" Mandy pointed to the T-shirt.

"*Why* did you get that?" Lila demanded.

"What, this?" Mr. Clark took off his sunglasses and glanced down at the lettering. "My I Am a Liar T-shirt?"

All of the Unicorns nodded in unison, unable to speak.

"Apparently someone placed a big order and never picked it up. The T-shirt shop was selling them for two dollars each. You know me—I can't resist a bargain!" Mr. Clark chuckled. "Of course, the sentiment's a bit off. But I think I can work with it. For instance, have I ever told you girls that you're very bad students?" He nodded. "Oops, there I go. I'm such a liar!" He chuckled some more.

Jessica turned to Lila, raising an eyebrow.

"And now I'm going to tell Mr. Bowman that he's fired!" Mr. Clark announced. Then he shook his head, laughing. "Whoops. I really am turning into quite a liar, aren't I?" He turned to go. "Goodbye, and have fun! You'll see me dancing later. Ha, ha, ha! I'm lying! I don't dance!"

As soon as Mr. Clark was out of earshot the Unicorns instinctively gathered in a tight circle. "Let's get one thing straight. We're not picking up those T-shirts," Janet stated firmly.

Everyone nodded in agreement.

"Repulsive," Lila said.

"Hideous," Ellen agreed with a shudder.

"But I'm willing to take it even one step further than that," Janet said. "Jessica, get me a pen."

Jessica rummaged in her knapsack and pulled out a pen. She handed it to Janet, along with a small notebook. "What are you going to write?"

"It's time to start a new petition," Janet declared. "No more ugly T-shirts with dumb slogans!" she jotted down.

Jessica took the pen back and scribbled her name on the first line. This was one promise she wouldn't have trouble keeping. And she didn't need to lie about it either.

Bantam Books in the SWEET VALLEY TWINS series.
Ask your bookseller for the books you have missed.

Surf's Up at Sweet Valley

Check out **Sweet Valley Online** when you're surfing the Internet!
It is *the* place to get the scoop on what's happening with your favorite twins,
Jessica and Elizabeth Wakefield, and the gang at Sweet Valley.
The official site features:

Sneak Peeks
Be the first to know all the juicy details of upcoming books!

Hot News
All the latest and greatest Sweet Valley news including
special promotions and contests.

Meet Francine Pascal
Find out about Sweet Valley's creator and send her a letter by e-mail!

Mailing List
Sign up for Sweet Valley e-mail updates and give us your feedback!

Bookshelf
A handy reference to the World of Sweet Valley.

★ ★

Check out Sweet Valley Online today!

http://www.sweetvalley.com